THE MAGIC CHARM

When Goldie Smith spies the portrait of the three Crosby girls for the first time, belonging to her dear Great-aunt Mary and painted long ago by an enigmatic local artist, she can't help but wonder at the history behind it. She also takes an instant shine to Rob Tyson, the handsome man who comes to photograph the painting. But his first love seems to be the rare birds he makes extensive trips to record with his camera. Is there room for Goldie in his life as well?

Books by Christina Green
in the Linford Romance Library:

CHRISTINA GREEN

THE MAGIC CHARM

Complete and Unabridged

LINFORD
Leicester

First published in Great Britain in 2017

First Linford Edition
published 2018

A catalogue record for this book is available
from the British Library.

ISBN 978–1–4448–3780–3

Published by
F. A. Thorpe (Publishing)
Anstey, Leicestershire

Set by Words & Graphics Ltd.
Anstey, Leicestershire
Printed and bound in Great Britain by
T. J. International Ltd., Padstow, Cornwall

This book is printed on acid-free paper

1

I was surprised to find a man in Great-aunt Mary's bedsitting room. I closed the door, met her welcoming smile and returned it, going across the room and hugging her.

'Hallo, Aunt Mary. Good to see you again. How are you?'

She sat up a little straighter. 'As well as I can be at my advanced age.' Her eyes twinkled. 'It's always lovely to see you, Goldie.' Looking away towards the man who stood there with a camera in his hand, she said, 'Marigold Smith is my niece, Mr Tyson.' She looked at me again. 'Mr Tyson is a photographer.'

'That's fairly obvious,' I said mischievously.

Aunt Mary frowned at me. 'Sit down, Goldie, and I'll tell you what's happening.' She nodded towards my usual Windsor chair by the far wall of her

1

small cosy room. 'And you, Mr Tyson, sit somewhere, too. I can't put up with people looking down at me all the time.'

Mr Tyson and I exchanged glances. I sat down and so did he, looking uncomfortable. I wondered why.

'Now,' said Aunt Mary, and I saw pleasure lighting her face, 'this is all about the three Crosby girls. Mr Tyson is here to photograph their portrait.'

At once I looked across the room to the wall behind her chair and saw the picture of the Crosby girls sitting neatly together in a room with open curtain-blown windows. They were all pretty, dark-haired with big blue ribbons tied in bows on the tops of their heads. Three young women. I smiled to myself, thinking that today they would be unruly teenagers but not in their days, which were, I supposed, years ago. These girls looked at the painter with expressionless faces. Although — was I imagining it? — their eyes were full of dreams and, no doubt, their own various thoughts.

2

Aunt Mary broke into my ruminations. 'The Crosby girls — Edwina, Rose and Harriet — were painted by the artist, their father, Charles Mason. Quite a famous name at the time.'

'What time, Aunt Mary? Long ago?'

She kept her eyes on the portrait and was silent for a moment or two. 'The days just before the Second World War.'

There was a silence while we all kept looking at the portrait. Then Aunt Mary said slowly, 'A long time ago indeed,' and I thought her hands were shaking in her lap.

Time to return to the present, I told myself warily, because I could see that these girls were upsetting her with perhaps forgotten memories. I shifted in my chair and looked at Tyson, sitting there with that large camera. 'So why are you here?' I asked baldly. 'To photograph my aunt, I suppose, and do a feature in the local paper about her coming up to her hundredth birthday?'

He looked at me, and I realised his eyes were a strange colour — dark green and blue, merging like the sea on a dull day. Suddenly I realised they matched his plain teal-coloured jersey. Then I looked at him properly — a youngish man, neatly dressed in jeans, an open-necked shirt and that nice jersey, and trainers that showed a bit of wear. His long legs were stretched out with the shoes on show, and I realised that he had no vanity.

Not bad, I thought. *And I like the hair.* Dark, with a heavy lock falling over his forehead. I decided to smile at him. 'Cat got your tongue?' I asked in a friendly voice.

Aunt Mary wasn't pleased. 'Goldie, behave yourself. Yes, Mr Tyson has taken a photo of me, and also of the Crosby girls.'

I frowned. 'Whatever for?'

Tyson turned to gaze at me. 'I do photos for the local paper in my spare time,' he said shortly.

Spare time? I thought. *Interesting.* I said, 'So what's your proper job?'

Again that tight-mouthed stare across

the room. 'I work as assistant curator in an art gallery. We're planning an exhibition of local artists in the autumn. I was surprised to find this beautiful Charles Mason here. And your aunt kindly agreed to me photographing it.'

'Why?'

His mouth tightened even more. 'To show my curator boss and see if she agrees that it would fit into the exhibition.'

Aunt Mary nodded, and I understood that she would like the painting of the Crosby girls to be seen by a larger and probably more appreciative audience than just herself and the staff of the Riverside Residential Home.

'OK,' I said breezily. 'I get the set-up. Where is this gallery — is it local?'

'In Exeter. We're hoping it will attract lots of people — and, of course, tourists.'

'Hmmm,' I said, 'Exeter without tourists is best, but I suppose we need the pennies they spend. Let me know when the exhibition is to be shown, and I'll bring Aunt Mary.'

'I'm not sure . . . ' she said in a frail voice.

I turned to her and grinned. 'We can take my car from here, and I can push a wheelchair up the Exeter streets. You'll be fine, dear Aunt Mary. I'm sure you'd like to go, wouldn't you?'

'Oh, I'd love it, Goldie. You see, I know a few things about those girls in the portrait, particularly their father — such a talented painter; and I'd so like to see people admiring it. Thank you, dear, for suggesting it.' Her smile was reward enough for an hour or so in the crowded city sometime in the future.

I glanced at my watch, got up, pushed the chair back against the wall and went to her, putting my arms around her. I kissed her cheek and she kissed mine. 'I'll be off now,' I said. 'It's nearly your lunchtime, and I've got a trip to Cornwall this afternoon.'

She smiled as I went towards the

door. 'Another of your holiday cottages to inspect, dear?'

'That's it. Apparently an upmarket one. Should be attractive — and expensive.' I glanced at Tyson, also standing up and cradling his camera in his arms. I felt he was watching me, so I said casually, 'Can I give you a lift anywhere, Mr Tyson? But I expect you have your own transport.'

He shifted from one foot to the other. 'Actually, no, I haven't,' he said, leaving me wondering why the lack of transport should make him sound so cross.

'Where do you live?'

He met my eyes with a frown. 'In Torquay — at the moment.'

We looked at each other, and I could read his thoughts. *Why does this wretched woman want to know so much about me?* Grinning to myself, I opened the door and stood there, glancing back over my shoulder. 'I'm on my way to Torquay right now — you're welcome to come if you want.'

He went to Aunt Mary's side and

held out his hand. She took it, smiling up into those strange sea-green eyes. 'I hope you'll come again, Mr Tyson, and that your curator will agree to adding the girls to your exhibition.'

I waited, wondering at how quickly he had changed his mood. No longer snappy, just quiet, and calmly putting Aunt Mary's hand gently back into her lap.

He smiled. 'I'll certainly be back, Mrs Seaton.'

Strange man, I told myself; and then we were out of the room and going downstairs.

He paused at the bottom while I headed for the front door. He didn't follow. I looked back and saw him speaking to Matron, who smiled nicely at him, nodded her head and said, 'Of course, Mr Tyson. I'll phone and tell you when the party is to be. I understand the local paper is keen to do a feature about Mrs Seaton. A hundred! Now that's really something wonderful; and such a delightful woman.

She has a few tales to tell, I'm sure!'

Tyson nodded. 'Indeed. And I hope she'll allow me to hear them sometime. Goodbye, Matron. I'll look forward to hearing from you. And, of course, coming to the party.'

I left the house and went rapidly towards my car. Why had I invited him to come with me? It was clear he was a journalist, only interested in writing the local news and gossip. Not at all the man I had thought him at first. And then he was getting in beside me, settling his camera on the seat behind before turning to look at me.

'This is kind of you, Miss Smith. I expected to take the bus, but with that big thing — ' He gestured back at the camera. ' — it's a lot to lug about.'

I didn't reply. I took the road to Torquay, wondering what sort of house he lived in. Why he didn't have a car. And did he really think I would let Matron invite him to the party? Such a momentous gathering would only be for family and close friends.

Well, I would make an excuse to Matron next time I saw her, and say that he was otherwise engaged. And then another thought came. What if he told me to mind my own business? I ground the gears as we approached the final roundabout, and saw him glance out of the window with a hint of amusement.

He had such a lean, beautifully boned face; tanned highlighted cheek-bones; and that dimple in his strong chin. I swerved unnecessarily to avoid a car that had given me signals that it was crossing into another lane, and I thought, *I'm behaving like a gauche schoolgirl. Damn the man. I'll be glad to get rid of him.*

Such unpleasant thoughts were inter-rupted in a few minutes as he raised a hand, pointing the way into a small street full of elderly-looking houses and a few rather ratty shops. Not Torquay at is best. I drew up at the bottom of a close, looked at him and said, 'Is this where you live? Not exactly the beautiful architecture Torquay is noted for, is it?'

He gave me a stare, and I watched a smile lift his straight lips. He grinned as if I had said something amusing. 'Yes, it's a bit dull, but I'll be moving along quite soon.'

I couldn't help the words that rushed into my head. 'Where are you going?'

Turning, he manhandled the big camera into his arms and opened the door, ready to get out. But I couldn't let him go like this — I might never see him again. I must find out where he would be moving to. I laid a hand on his arm. 'At least give me your new address. I'll need to send you an invitation to Aunt Mary's party.'

His smile was smooth and slightly amused again. 'I'll be around,' he said, and got out of the car. 'Thanks for the lift. See you sometime — Miss Smith.' And off he went, stopping at one of the worst dwelling places in the whole street and unlocking the door, his beloved camera still held

11

safely in both arms.

I sat there, almost mesmerised by my churning mind. What a strange man. And why had I got so involved with him? Of course I wouldn't send him an invitation. What had I been thinking of? I drove off, stopping eventually in the car park below the handsome building where I worked. I felt bemused, cross with myself, but eager to know a bit more about Mr Tyson.

Nick Burns, my boss, poked his head around the doorway into my tiny cluttered office. He lifted heavy dark eyebrows at me, his voice accusing. 'There you are, Goldie. I thought you'd got lost somewhere. Look, I've got a message from the woman who owns the Cornish place.'

'I'm going there as soon as I've had my lunch, Nick. Allow me time to have a quick sandwich and a coffee, will you?'

He frowned. 'Why do you always make me out to be a monster? I don't bully you, do I?'

'Only when I've done something wrong. And I love you really, Nick.' I grinned, put my phone into my bag, got up and stood beside him. Then I looked at him properly. Usually we were so busy discussing business matters, and arguing, that I never saw him as an individual, just as my boss. He was middle height, a bit on the soon-to-be-paunchy side, but with such a kind face that at times I really couldn't understand why he snapped at me.

'Love me, eh? Well, you've got a funny way of showing it, Goldie. But I know you've got some odd ideas about men.'

We looked at each other for a stretching moment, and I immediately remembered how my ex, Mark, had loved me and then left me. Was there any wonder I didn't trust men now, or didn't want a new relationship? I made a big decision, pushed away the unhappy thoughts, and grinned at Nick. 'Sorry. I do try.'

He grunted and stepped away,

heading for his own office. 'We've said that amazing word 'love' a few times — but it doesn't seem to get us anywhere, does it? OK then, Goldie, on your way — and bring back the contract for that nice expensive house on the beach, won't you?'

I nodded. 'You bet I will, Nick. Cheers for now.' I marched out of the office, feeling his eyes on me as I waited for the lift and then got inside.

Cornwall, as usual, welcomed me. Straight over the Tamar and then on towards the sea. I discovered I was feeling excited, and then memories of my childhood holidays returned, and I smiled foolishly as I turned up the drive to the house built almost on the edge of the cliff at St Methyr.

What a wonderful holiday home this would be. It had a small garden, but tall tamarisk trees nodded quite happily in the wind blowing off the sea, and I could imagine parties taking place here. Glasses being lifted, chatter all around, elegant clothes and some beautiful food presented on a long table decorated with flowers. *Hmm*, I thought, *wouldn't mind being here for a holiday myself.* A crazy dream, of course, but I'd always had a lively imagination.

Then, as I parked the car, got out and walked to the front door, I had a sudden mad thought. It would be nice to have a man here to share my dream. Mark was long gone. I knew Nick fancied me, but I had no romantic feelings for him. Another face, another name ... Tyson? Oh yes, he would enjoy all this — taking photographs, and telling me a bit more about himself. Now, that would be nice ...

I rang the bell and a woman answered. Wispy grey brown hair framed her lined face, and there was a welcoming smile and a thick Devon burr in her quiet voice. 'Good afternoon, Miss Smith. Do come in.' She led me into a large airy room with huge windows that were full of views of the sea below, and pulled out a comfortable-looking chair for me to sit in. I put my briefcase at my feet and wondered exactly who she was. Not the owner, but perhaps a relative of the owner?

As if she read my thoughts, she said comfortably, 'I'm the caretaker, but I expect you know that. I live in one of the old coastguard cottages on the headland over there.' She pointed to the window towards the land stretching out to sea beyond the beach below, and I saw two buildings right on the cliff edge.

I nodded at her as I began taking papers from my case and said, 'Yes, we were told that Cliff House was being looked after by someone local. It's nice to meet you, Mrs, er — ?'

As she moved towards the door, she looked back and chuckled. 'Call me Flo. I were born Florence, but what a mouthful! Now, tea or coffee, Miss Smith? Then we can get down to business — something about a contract, I believe?'

Warmth ran through me. I liked Flo

at once. 'Coffee, please,' I said with a smile. 'No milk or sugar.'

'That sounds horrid,' she said with a grin. 'But if that's what you want.' She left the room, and soon came back with a tray and that friendly smile. She put the mug of coffee on a small table beside me and then sat on the long chesterfield facing me. 'Well,' she said, sipping from her own mug, 'what can I tell you, Miss Smith? But then, I expect you know most of it. I mean, the solicitor dealing with the will must have told you — did he?'

I wondered what secrets were about to be spilled. 'I know there's a law case going on about who the house was left to when the original owner died, but that's all. Except that the solicitor recommended renting the house to holidaymakers, at least until the new owner takes over. And that's why I'm here.' I produced the contract Nick had drawn up, found a pen and went to sit beside her on the sofa. 'This simply says you agree to continue being a caretaker here, and to look after Cliff House this summer while holiday visitors come and go.'

She took the paper and pen, but looked doubtful. 'Well, I suppose that'll be all right. Only, I don't want this lovely old house to be spoiled or messed up, because you never know about holidaymakers, do you?'

I smiled reassuringly. 'That's our job, Flo. My boss is keen that Cliff House remain exactly as it is. There shouldn't be any problems for you, except perhaps to welcome holidaymakers, and then see that when they leave everything is where it should be.'

She laughed and took the pen. 'Well, that sounds all right. Thank you, Miss Smith. Of course I'll sign. On this line, is it?'

I watched her write her name carefully: Florence Bailey, with a big 'Mrs' after it. 'Thank you,' I said. 'That's fine. And my boss, Nick Burns, will also sign it and send you a copy. And of course we'll let you know when the first holidaymakers are due to arrive.'

We looked at each other and smiled; and then, a bit regretfully because I was finding Cliff House to be a warm, welcoming sort of place, I put away the paper and got to my feet. I said, 'Thanks for the coffee, Flo, and I'm sure we'll meet again before too long.'

She saw me off with her big grin and waved as I drove away. At the top of the road there was a parking place, so I stopped there and simply looked down at the sea. It danced in the sunlight, with small white waves bubbling along as it rolled towards the scalloped edge of the beach. It was all I could do to get out and walk along that golden beach — but business called, and I just hoped, as I'd said, I would be here again before too long.

2

The next day, Nick and I discussed the
contract for Cliff House at St Methyr
and the law case that was going on,
trying to trace the new owner. 'These
lawyers take their time,' he complained,
and then grinned, sitting back in his
chair. 'So that's fine — the contract's
been signed, and I'll countersign it and
send her a copy.' He looked up at me
doubtfully. 'This caretaker — what's
she like? Up to the job, I hope?'

Flo was in my mind — her warm
voice, that big grin, and the feeling I
had about her that she would do her
job very well indeed. I didn't want Nick
being suspicious of her, so I said
sharply, 'She's an efficient woman. The
house is beautiful, and I know she cares
for it. I'm sure she's good with people
— well, she was with me.'

He gave me one of his amused

smiles. 'She's got you on her side, has she? Goldie, you'll never make a good businessperson. You're far too soft, you know.'

That was too much. I got to my feet, and he looked up at me, his eyes amused; but there was something else in them that worried me. Then he said almost apologetically, 'You're right. I'm wrong. Let's agree to compromise. So how about having a meal with me tonight?'

I thought about what that meant. Meeting for a drink, talking shop, and then becoming friendlier in his nice flat and hoping that the cooking course he was doing would produce an edible meal. But something came out quickly before I realised what I was saying: 'Sorry, Nick. Other things to do tonight, but perhaps another time.'

Then I felt ashamed of myself, for he looked at me almost sorrowfully, I thought. My mind whirled. Why had I said that? I had nothing to do this evening except clean my flat and perhaps sort out some washing. I walked to the door, but something made me turn back and give him a warm smile. 'Sorry,' I repeated, 'but sometime next week would be great. Cheers for now, Nick.' Not waiting for an answer, I went down in the lift, got into my car and drove home.

The flat seemed cheerless and lonely, so I was delighted when the phone rang and a woman's voice said, 'Marigold Smith? This is Donna Adams, curator of the Exeter Art Gallery. The Matron at your great-aunt's residential home gave me your number. Could we meet to discuss her portrait of the Crosby girls?'

At once, I thought this was the result of the Tyson man's photograph. But I was interested. 'Yes, of course,' I said. 'Friday afternoon this week would suit me. Would that be all right for you?'

She paused for a moment, and I imagined her checking her diary. 'That would be fine,' she said more briskly. 'I look forward to meeting you at the

Riverside Home. Shall we say 2.30?'

'Yes. And I'll tell my great-aunt to expect us. She generally has a sleep in the afternoon, but I think your visit will keep her awake!'

She did not answer my jokey comment; just said, 'I'll see you there, Ms Smith. Goodbye for now.'

The line went dead, and I was left thinking hard. So the Tyson photograph had interested this woman from the art gallery. Well, it interested me, too. I would ring Matron and ask her to prepare Great-aunt Mary for our visit. I had an instinctive feeling that she would be happy to talk about the famous Crosby girls. And I would be just as happy to hear what she had to say. The words 'to share her memories' suddenly filled my mind, and I returned to the pile of washing with a smile and a feeling of something interesting coming into my lonely life.

Friday came and I was filled with some excitement, wondering how Aunt

Mary would feel about the photograph of the Crosby girls. At 2.30 sharp I was in her room at Riverside, waiting for Donna Adams to arrive. There was a tap on the door, and Matron ushered her in. She was small, a fragile-looking blond dressed in a Victorian sort of dress with long sleeves and a high neck. I stared, but of course it suited her. It was dark green, which emphasised her green-grey eyes, and the maxi-length skirt made her look taller and authoritative. She had a good smile, and at once I felt happy to be here with her and Aunt Mary. I had expected from her phone call that she might be much the arty lady I had imagined, but her greeting to us both was friendly, almost warm.

'Mrs Seaton, I'm so glad to meet you. And Ms Smith. Good of you to come today. From my own experience, I know that Fridays are busy days; clearing up for the weekend and all that.'

Aunt Mary smiled and so did I. I

think we both felt relieved that here was someone we could be friendly with despite our lack of knowledge about portraits and the arts. We sat down, and she took a folded sheet of newspaper from her bag. 'This is the photo of you, Mrs Seaton, and of your portrait,' she said, offering them to Aunt Mary. 'I hope you'll be pleased with it. I think Rob Tyson did his usual good job, but one never knows how people will feel about being in the paper.'

I was glad of the silence that followed; Aunt Mary was looking at her photos, and my head was buzzing. Rob Tyson — yes, a name I could be pleased with.

The Aunt Mary said, 'Goodness, don't I look old?' and at once I went to her and put my arms around her.

'Darling Aunt Mary, you *are* old! But it doesn't matter, because inside you're still young and lovely.'

Donna Adams chipped in, 'We're all getting older, Mrs Seaton; but I think this photo makes you look just what you are — elderly but at peace with your world.'

Aunt Mary looked at her, and then a smile lit her face. 'Thank you,' she said simply. 'How right you are, my dear. Yes, I am quite contented with my life — although, of course . . . ' Her smile faded and a note of anxiety sounded in her voice. 'Although there are some memories that haunt me still.'

I drew my chair closer to her and took her hands. 'Perhaps if you talk about them, Aunt Mary, they might lose some of their hold over you.' We looked at each other for a long moment, and then I summoned the courage to ask, 'Are your memories do to with the Crosby girls? But surely those elegant young ladies never did anything awful, did they? In this picture they look as if butter wouldn't melt in their pretty rosebud mouths!' As I hoped, this wild surmise brought a smile to Aunt Mary's face; and when she spoke, her voice was firm and steady again.

'Goldie, you have such an imagination. But, you know, you were half right — one of the Crosby girls did misbehave.'

Donna and I exchanged glances, and she said, 'I'd love to hear about that, Mrs Seaton. Could you bring yourself to tell us what happened?'

'Well . . . ' Aunt Mary thought for a moment and then sat back in her chair, smiling a little unhappily as she began her story. 'You see, they were much under their father's rule. They weren't allowed any freedom — always at home doing things young ladies did in those days . . . ' Her smile returned and she sat back more easily in her chair. Her bright eyes looked at Donna and then me. 'Painting wild flowers,' she said, her smile growing. 'Learning to play the piano — and I remember that Harriet asked for a violin but her father said no. And they all had sweet voices, so they sang in the evenings.'

I asked, 'Did you visit them, Aunt

Mary? You seem to have known them so well.'

She looked at me and I saw the smile fading. 'Yes. My mother was some sort of distant cousin to the family, and so we saw them quite often. We were a happy family then.'

I was caught. 'Do go on, Aunt Mary — it all sounds wonderful.'

'Yes, my dear, it was. But then the war came and everything changed.'

'The war, which started in 1939 when you were all so young and happy. What happened then?' I asked, but then wished I had kept quiet. Aunt Mary's eyes shone with tears and she turned her head away from our enquiring faces. I said quickly, 'Never mind, Aunt Mary; not if it upsets you. Let's talk about something else.'

But she wiped away the tears and looked at me with a new strength about her. 'Of course we must talk about it,' she said almost sharply. 'Because that's when it all started to happen, you see. Yes, during the war.'

28

A silence fell, and I realised her mind was busy with memories. Some of them must have been sad, of course; but surely there had been happiness, too?

Donna broke the silence. 'Could you possibly tell us what the Crosby girls did in the war, Mrs Seaton? Without troubling yourself too much?'

Aunt Mary took a deep breath, turned in her chair with both photos on her lap, and looked at the portrait behind her. After another moment's pause, she looked at us, and now her eyes were shining.

'They did what all we women did at that time,' she said. 'We found ourselves suitable, useful jobs, and went to war, too.'

3

I was intrigued. I had never thought about the war. That was something a long way off — yes, terrible, of course — which had threatened our country over sixty years ago. But Aunt Mary said all women worked and were in the middle of the war, like their men. It was a sobering thought. What sort of work had she done? And the Crosby girls — lovely, spoilt no doubt, and under their father's rule . . . had they found jobs, too? If so, what did they do? But Aunt Mary had slumped back in her chair and closed her eyes.

Donna and I signalled to each other. It was time to go. We got up, and she went to the door and half-opened it while I knelt by Aunt Mary's side and whispered, 'Thank you for all those memories, dear Aunt Mary. Perhaps we could hear more of them another day.

But for now we'll leave you in peace.' I looked at my watch and said more cheerfully, 'Time for your nap, and then it'll be teatime.' I joined Donna at the doorway and we both smiled as we said our goodbyes.

Walking along the passage, Donna said, 'She's an amazing woman. And yes, we must somehow get some more stories out of her. It would be wonderful to be able to put that lovely portrait into a living frame. Shall we meet again next week?'

I nodded. 'I'll be here, but I'll be in touch with her before that, just in case she's having second thoughts about remembering.'

We stopped in the car park, and I was unlocking the door when she called across to me. 'Don't go — I forgot to give you this.' She came to my side, looking slightly embarrassed and holding out something in her hand.

I took it, mystified, said 'Thanks,' and got into the car. Then something made me unfold the envelope she had given me and look at it. Inside was a small business card; I had no idea who had sent it to me. But then, looking at it more carefully, I saw the smallest picture of a bird in flight on the side of the card, and then a name and address beneath it.

Robert Tyson. The Studio, Castle Court, Exeter. A phone number, and then in strong handwriting, a message: *Marigold Smith — my address, if you want it.*

I let the card drop into my lap and stared through the windscreen with blind eyes. After a few minutes of deep thought, I let all the confusing ideas in my head rush out with a burst of excitement. It was from Rob. He had told me his address. And surely that was a sort of invitation. To phone him? Or — I gasped, and knew I was smiling — even to go and see him.

A decision quickly banished all other thoughts. Of course I would go to Exeter. Sometimes we had business there, and Nick needn't know if I took half an hour off and call on him. Rob. Robert Tyson. And he called me Marigold.

I drove home in a sort of happy daze, and it was only when I got into the flat that I started asking myself why I felt so excited. I had no answer, but I found myself smiling a lot.

I didn't get into Exeter with a bit of time to spare until the following week. But the excitement was still there. Having parked, I walked up Castle Court and found a plain oak doorway with a small sign on it. It said 'The Studio', and I pressed the bell, suddenly wondering what he would think about finding me on his doorstep. I hoped he would be pleased.

But when the door opened, I was looking at an elderly man with big bushy eyebrows and an untidy beard to match. He said, 'Yes?' in a deep voice, and I felt all the excitement drain out of me. This wasn't Rob. Had he given me this address as a joke, or even as a notice that he wasn't interested in me?

I held my breath for a moment, and then the words came out in a rush. 'Is Robert Tyson here? He — er — sent me this address . . .'

The man raised those terrifying eyebrows and looked if he wanted to smile but couldn't be bothered. 'Yes, he lives here,' he said, and I thought that deep voice was trying to get rid of me. That set my mind working. I wouldn't be used like this. I raised my head an inch higher and looked into his rather faded unblinking eyes with all the courage I could muster.

'When will he be in?' I asked. 'And could you give him a message that I was here? Marigold Smith.'

The eyebrows settled down and a faint smile appeared. 'A pretty name for a pretty woman,' he said. 'He won't be back for a couple of days. Got time off to go to Shetland and photograph the birds.'

'Photograph the birds?' My voice was raised, my face taut with surprise. What birds, for goodness sake? And then I remembered the small picture of a seagull of some sort on the top of the card he had sent me. I understood, and was able to smile at the man regarding me with a slight grin lighting up his hairy face.

'Aye, the birds,' he said, and the grin spread. 'The feathered ones. Back by the end of the week, he said. Yes, I'll tell him you were here.' He looked at me curiously. 'Does he know where to find you?' he asked, and I came down to earth again. I scrabbled in my bag, found my card with name, address and a phone number on it, and handed it over.

We smiled at each other, and then he said, 'Good luck, then,' and closed the door. Left on the doorstep, I took a deep breath, told myself to calm down, and went back to my car. Good luck, I thought. Yes, I definitely needed some.

Donna and I visited Aunt Mary the next Friday. After a warm welcome, she began talking about the celebrations for her hundredth birthday. Apparently

Riverside was going to town with their plans. 'First of all, a coffee party in the morning when the owner of the home and all the staff will be there, together with someone from the local paper. And then . . . ' Her smile grew. 'And then . . . '

She paused, and I said quickly, 'You'll need a rest after that, Aunt Mary.'

'I certainly will. And especially if I have a glass of sherry!'

Smiling, Donna said, 'I hope there'll be a grand lunch. What about the menu, Mrs Seaton? Have they told you what to expect?'

Aunt Mary straightened her shoulders and her smile grew. 'Yes, indeed. Cook tells me it's to be a leg of lamb — my favourite — with mint sauce and redcurrant jelly and lots of vegetables. I'll enjoy that.'

I thought a bit. 'And then the tea party, I suppose. With a marvellous cake.'

Donna cut in, 'And you'll have a card

from the Queen! Well, it sounds a really wonderful day, Mrs Seaton. And I know all your family and friends will enjoy being with you.'

Aunt Mary said quickly, 'Yes, indeed. I hope you'll come, Miss Adams. And what about the young man who took such a good photo of me? I should like to meet him again and thank him.'

I thought, *So Rob will be here. I'll see him and talk to him. Ask him about the birds* . . . I felt my grin grow into a proper warm smile.

Then I saw that Aunt Mary's smile had faded as she half-turned in her chair and looked up at the portrait of the Crosby girls. She said, half to herself, 'A pity those girls couldn't be here with me. How they would have loved a good party.'

Donna and I looked at each other, and she said gently, 'I believe you were fond of them. Perhaps you could tell us a little more about them, Mrs Seaton? You mentioned they all had jobs during the war. I've been looking at some archives we have in the gallery, showing women at work in those days.'

I wondered if this was too much to expect of Aunt Mary along with the excitement of her coming party. But no; she nodded, smiled at Donna and said slowly, 'Yes, we all did strange work — for without the men at home, it was up to us women to help things along. I expect your archives can make the past live again. Well, I can add a little to that. And yes, I'll tell you what we all did. Edwina followed her father's advice and became a VAD. As I remember, she'd always loved dressing up as a nurse and treating her sick dolls! Of course, he expected her to become trained and climb the ladder to a position like commandant, but I'm afraid Edwina did no such thing; instead she went to France as an ambulance driver. She was there near the front line, treating all those poor men who were wounded by the German shelling.'

There was a silence, and Donna and I looked at Aunt Mary with alarm. She was huddled in her chair, clearly lost in memories. I wondered guiltily if we had asked too much of her — thinking back, I knew, could be like opening Pandora's box, for you never knew what you would find there. And perhaps bringing the horrors of the war into her old mind had evoked only sadness. But then she looked up at us, straightened herself in her chair and gave us a big, wide grin. 'And, would you believe it, at the end of the war she was awarded a medal of some sort, for her bravery under fire.'

I heard Donna heave a big sigh of relief, and I did the same. So the story about Edwina had ended happily — thank goodness! Between us, we managed a little chuckle and I realised that Donna, like me, felt things deeply.

Then, out of the blue, I heard Nick's voice in my mind saying things about me being soft. This lit a small patch of anger within me, and I said, looking into Aunt Mary's faded eyes, 'Just shows, doesn't it, Aunt, that women aren't the softies men think them. The war must have opened up a new world for women. And we're still working at it.'

Aunt Mary nodded, but I didn't think she heard my words, for her face still had that nostalgic expression. But Donna understood. 'How right you are, Marigold,' she said. 'That sort of war still goes on. I had terrible difficulty in making myself curator of the gallery.' Her smile was warm and slightly amused. 'And I still get nasty comments from certain members of my staff.'

'Do you? That's terrible.' My mind jumped and something made me add, 'But surely not from Rob?' I felt colour mounting in my cheeks and added hastily, 'I mean your assistant curator, Robert Tyson.'

She was openly smiling now. 'Just call him Rob; we all do. No, he's above that petty sort of sniping-at-women thing. He's a nice man, and I'll be glad when he comes back from this photo shoot in Scotland.'

I held my breath and then asked, 'When will that be?'

Donna looked at me. I could feel that she understood my excitement; and it dawned on me that she, too, felt an attraction to Rob Tyson. 'On Tuesday,' she said briefly. 'And he'll be busy — we have so much to do, organising this exhibition.'

Was that a warning not to bother him? Not even to call on him and ask about the birds?

She made no reply, but looked back at Aunt Mary and said, 'Thank you so much, Mrs Seaton. May I come again next week? I'd love to hear how Edwina got on.'

But my aunt's eyes were closed, and she had leaned back in her chair. Obviously she had had enough for one afternoon, so I stepped towards the door, looked back at Donna and said firmly, 'Time to go, I think. See you next week, then.'

I kissed Aunt Mary goodbye and then left the room, knowing that Donna was following down the passage; but I wasn't in the mood to wait for her to catch up and talk. No longer could I think of her as a possible friend, for I realised how fond of Rob she sounded, which must surely mean I had no chance of seeing him or talking to him. Of being friendly and wondering how things might go from now on. No, with just a few words Donna had put an end to all that.

4

Driving home, I thought about what Donna had said — that women still had to fight to get anywhere; and I wondered if what she had experienced in fighting for her career had given her a thicker skin than I had thought. If so, I could only admire her and step back.

Those thoughts brought me to a decision. I would call on Robert Tyson and find out what he was like without listening to Donna's vague words. On Friday he would come home from Scotland. I would give him a day or two to get himself straight again, and then I would drive round and say, 'Hello, Rob. Thanks for letting me know this new address. Can I come in? I'd love to see some of your photographs.'

But it didn't turn out quite like that. I put on clean jeans and a favourite top and drove into Exeter. First of all, I found all the car parks full, so I had to park quite a distance away and then walk through the town up to Castle Court. It was a hot day, so arriving at The Studio, I felt sunburned and rather untidy; but I pressed the bell and took deep breaths to calm myself down.

Steps approached, and a hand opened the door — but not Rob's. I looked into the faded eyes of the bearded man who I recognised from my visit last week. I opened my mouth to ask politely if Rob was in, but he got there first.

'Oh, it's you again. Want to see the lad, I suppose, do you? Well, he's out.'

I stared at him. Really, what a non-welcome. I almost wished I hadn't bothered to come.

But then there was suddenly some-one at my elbow, and that deep voice saying, 'Marigold — good to see you. Come in.' It was Rob, with a heavy backpack that he was unslinging as he looked at me. And he was smiling. 'You look rather warm. I expect Gus has got some of his homemade lemonade. Please, go in.'

I stepped into the rather dark, narrow hall, and saw Gus opening the door and nodding at me as if to say I was welcome. I entered the room opening out before me — a kitchen. It was untidy, and there was some washing up waiting to be done; but there was a warmth about it, as if were a much-loved room. That made me smile to myself. Turning, I saw Rob come in, settle his pack on the long littered table and grin at the man he called Gus, who produced a jug of lemonade, found some glasses, and then looked at me.

'Well, don't just stand there — take a seat. And if you need some more sugar, say so.'

The lemonade was excellent, and I smiled at the bearded face that looked at me with such interest. 'It's good,' I said. 'No need for more sugar, thank you.'

Gus turned and looked at Rob, who was busy unpacking groceries. 'No manners,' he said in his throaty voice. 'Introduce me, will you?'

Rob put the last packet on the table and stood up straight. He smiled at me and said with amusement in his voice, 'Marigold, this is Augustus Grayling.' The grin became a smile. 'Actually, he's my uncle. He likes everyone to call him Gus.'

The man held out a large hand and looked deep into my eyes. 'Marigold. Now there's a name and a half. Shorten it, surely, do you?'

'Yes,' I said, answering his smile. 'I'm just Goldie.'

'Goldie Smith,' said Rob, picking up his glass of lemonade and taking a long drink. 'We met at Mrs Seaton's home when I was photographing her.'

'And the Crosby girls,' I added quickly.

Rob put down the empty glass and looked at me for a moment. 'Yes, the Crosby girls. My boss, Donna Adams, has told me that Mrs Seaton has some fascinating tales to tell about the girls during the last war. She hopes to gather some more, which will bring life to the portrait when it's exhibited.'

I sipped the last drop of that excellent lemonade and waited for him to speak again. In my mind I told myself that he had seen Donna since his return, and felt a pang of jealousy. But his voice was quiet and warm when he added, 'I'd love to visit Mrs Seaton again. Are you likely to be seeing her this week, Goldie?'

I was Goldie to him now. My smile grew. 'Lovely,' I said easily. 'I'll be going on Wednesday — I have a bit of work to do first, so I'll be seeing her at tea time. Four o'clock, usually.' We looked at each other with growing interest. 'I'm sure you'll be welcome, and she can talk to you about your portrait.'

He nodded. 'And perhaps tell me some more about those elegant young girls.'

My mind was busy. Yes, he had taken the photograph; but was it Donna who had asked him to visit my great-aunt in

47

the hope that she would tell more tales? I frowned as my thoughts became more involved, and he noticed.

'What are you thinking? You look worried.'

I caught my breath. Here was a man who knew about feelings — so different from others I had known. Others I thought I had loved. I said, 'Not really worried. Just wondering if Aunt Mary's ready to go back into her memories again.'

He nodded, and then sat back in his chair. 'I know what you mean. Memories can be difficult, can't they? Well, if we go, perhaps we can just talk about the photo in the paper and her coming birthday. What do you think?'

I smiled and felt my worries fading fast. 'I think that's a splendid idea, Rob. I'll go along with that. And if she should chose to talk about the Crosby girls, well, then . . . '

He got up, came round to my chair, put his hands on the back, and said seemingly just to me, 'We'll play it by ear. And now, come upstairs — I want you to see Gus's paintings.'

Gus, standing by the sink, regarding the washing-up that awaited him, turned and looked at me. His voice held a touch of fierceness. 'Don't expect too much. Daubs, most of them. But well, that's a long time ago, and I'm still trying to do better.'

Rob put a hand on my arm. 'Don't believe a word of that,' he said in my ear. 'Come and see for yourself.'

I didn't say anything, for the whole afternoon had taken on a new sort of feeling, leaving me excited and rather happy. I felt welcome in this untidy, dark and neglected old house. Something was making me wonder what the paintings — daubs, he had said — were really like. And why was Rob living here? Why had he moved from that awful little house in Torquay? Why no transport of his own? Why had he gone to Scotland? I hoped I would see some of his own photographs, besides Gus's work.

We went up the narrow, badly lit stairs and then into a huge room where the light streamed in from two big uncurtained windows, and I remembered what I'd been taught at school by the painting mistress: *Light from a north window, that's what you need.*

One painting, larger than others propped against the wall, caught my eye, and I gasped. I moved without realising and went up to this picture. It was a sunset view looking out to sea. There were black rocks with white waves foaming around them, and the sun in its splendour, shading from fiery red through ochre, turquoise and finally to shadowy pearl-grey. In the middle was a child running through the sand and lacy waves.

It was a beautiful picture, expertly painted, and full of feeling. Turning, I looked into Rob's watchful sea-green eyes. 'It's wonderful,' I whispered. 'How could he possibly call it a daub?'

Rob nodded his head, and quietly so that I almost didn't hear, said, 'It's his childhood come to life again. That's him on the beach, feet in the water.'

I looked again, and then asked, 'Where is it? Such a lovely place.'

'His old home. See the house above, on the cliff edge? Well, that's where he was born and brought up. He insists that his work is only just a daub, but I think he's trying to forget something in his life. He's always painting that beach, so I suppose it brings back memories and perhaps helps to make the past less painful.'

I nodded, thinking of Aunt Mary and her memories. I turned to look at Rob. 'Sometimes it's best not to go back.' I saw his eyes shut tight for a moment before opening again and turning away. As if he couldn't talk about memories, I thought.

Then I remembered I was here to see photographs. 'I'd love to see some of your work, Rob,' I said hopefully.

He smiled at me. 'From the sublime to the ridiculous! Well, if you must. Over here.'

He led me across the big bare room, past a small dais with a hard chair on it, past the stand that held Gus's latest painting; but I didn't bother to look. I wanted to see the photographs.

5

Rob stood at my side and looked at the wall, which was covered in bird life. It was all so unexpected that I caught my breath. 'Birds!' I whispered, looking at him and seeing a new gleam in those wonderful eyes.

'Yes, birds. They're my passion, so I photograph them wherever I am.'

Things began to make sense. 'Scotland, for example?' I asked, and he nodded. 'And the bird printed on your business card, of course. But why didn't you tell me before?'

He smiled. 'You didn't ask.'

'No.' What a fool I had been, dreaming dreams about him and only now finding out the truth. His passion. I smiled at him apologetically. 'You must have thought me a fool, Rob. I mean, I guessed you were off doing something amazing, but I had no idea about the birds.'

He half-turned and picked up a board lying on a chair. 'I've been mad about them since childhood. And then, when I discovered the magic of cameras . . . well, that was it.'

I was driven to look at the photograph mounted on the board he held; something inside of me said that this was important. I looked at the huge brown-bodied bird with open black-fringed wings, photographed in a magnificent pose, full of movement as it opened its wings wide and swooped down — possibly after prey, I guessed. Bemused, I asked, 'This is an eagle of some kind, isn't it? Such wonderful colours — that beautiful shape with feathers catching the sunlight and shining. Rob, it's a beautiful photograph. You must feel proud of it.'

He took me by the arm and led me across the room to another wall full of birdlife. Swallows on the wing, wrens with their fidgety tails — I could almost see them moving — and a robin with that familiar gleaming bright eye, looking at me as if I were the photographer himself. And then the mighty kite, a heron scooping up its breakfast by shining water, and — I smiled as I saw it — a mother duck leading her trail of tiny ducklings towards a distant pond.

They were all alive, taking me back to my early love of nature, something I had forgotten in the wild race to earn a living. I turned to Rob and said, my voice quiet and full of admiration, 'You're a real artist — I mean an ornithologist, don't I? Something like that. Rob, you have such talent. Thank you so much for showing me all these wonderful photos.'

He just nodded, and then walked back to the large photo of the eagle. He scanned it, then turned and looked at me. 'This is the one,' he said quietly. 'I'm entering it for a national competition. If it wins, I'll be made. If not, well . . . ' The sentence remained unfinished.

'If not, what?'

He shrugged. 'Go back to being an unemployed chap with a camera, I suppose. Wish me luck, Goldie, won't you?'

I found no words to answer, but my thoughts flew. Such talent, such a love for natural creatures — of course he must win the competition!

The door opened and Gus appeared. 'Looking at the birds, are you? Yes, of course, they're good. Real atmosphere, and caught in the most attractive poses; but nothing to match a seaside view.' Grinning, he walked across the room and stared at his beautiful picture.

I went and stood beside him. 'It really is lovely, Gus. Where is it? Somewhere you lived as a child?'

He turned and looked at me, then back at the picture. 'My childhood home. A house on the cliff. The beach, and nature at its easiest and best. I spent hours there.'

I felt an instinctive need to find our more, so asked him — casually, I hoped, 'Where is this, Gus? Looks like Cornwall.'

He gave a sigh and looked at me before turning away and going towards Rob, who stood beside his birds covering the wall. 'A place called Cliff House.'

His words reached me as if in a dream, and I hardly heard myself ask, 'Near the village of St Methyr?'

He was clearly surprised at the question, but he simply said, 'Know it, do you?' And I was left wondering how to tell him about the contract recently signed to let out Cliff House to holidaymakers for the next few weeks.

I turned away quickly, lest he should see from my expression that I knew about his old home. It was Rob who came to the rescue, looking intently me and then saying, 'Would you like a stroll through the gardens, Goldie? Beautiful trees and plants there.'

I paused and thought. He must have noticed I was upset, and this was his way of trying to help me out of whatever problem it was that I had encountered. Among all the other thoughts crowding in on me, one seemed strong and important. He was a compassionate man who wanted to help people. So I managed a smile and said, 'That's a wonderful idea, Rob. Yes, please, let's go.'

Gus watched us leave the studio, muttering things I didn't hear properly as we went downstairs and out into Castle Court. As we walked into the castle gardens, I calmed down and said, 'Was Gus complaining about us leaving?'

Rob shook his head. 'He's a law unto himself. Got a few problems, Gus has.' Then he looked at me and grinned. 'He's not the only one, either. But never mind. Do you know about these old gardens?'

I wondered just what he meant. Well, everybody had problems, I told myself, but I didn't think I could ask about his. So I returned to what we were doing, and where we were. We went through what remained of the old castle gate and into the stretching gardens that surrounded the moat, now filled with a dark canopy of trees, and making the colourful flowers in the big beds stand out. 'Such a lovely place,' I said quietly, and looked at him beside me.

For a moment his face was tight, and I thought he looked worried. But then, meeting my eyes, he smiled and said, 'Yes; nature at her best. Trees, flowers and shrubs, and a world of birdsong.'

'And benches to sit on.' I led the way to a bench from where I could see the old wall connecting Northernhay Gardens with these, Rougement, the ancient castle the Normans had built and named after the rich red soil of Devon.

We sat in silence and looked around in the quiet of the approaching evening. A few people walked along the various paths and then disappeared. A grey squirrel leaped over the grass, looking at us and pausing, as if expecting crumbs or other bits of the many picnics that were eaten here in this lovely spot.

Rob took his mobile phone out of his pocket and managed to film the squirrel before it shot off into the nearest tree. He looked at me and grinned. 'Never let a likely subject go without filming it,' he said. And suddenly he was taking a picture of me — with my mouth half-open and wondering eyes, I thought, amused and also intrigued.

'Don't waste film on me,' I said, aware of the feeling growing between us. 'Keep it for your birds.'

He didn't say anything, but put his mobile back into his pocket. He asked, 'Are you interested in hearing about Gus's problems, Goldie?'

I nodded, wanting to add, 'And yours, too,' but knowing I must take this quietly. 'If you think I can help in resolving them, Rob.' Our eyes met, and I saw his were dark and intent.

'He won't mind my telling you. Gus is one of those people who talk all the time about their life and problems.' Now he was smiling and sitting more comfortably on the bench, with only a small space between us. Something warm and pleasurable spread through me, and I thought briefly that this was a lovely way to spend a summer evening.

'All right, fire away,' I said, and waited to hear what bothered poor old Gus.

'Well . . . ' For a moment I thought Rob had run out of words, but then he looked at me and said slowly, 'It's a question of an inheritance. You see, Gus's elder brother died last year, and because my father's missing, there's a problem with granting him the inheritance. He worries about it all the time, and I've noticed in the last few weeks that he's become more and more impatient about how long the court is taking.'

I was surprised. Into my mind came an image of the house on the cliff that should belong to Gus if the lawyers sorted themselves out. But I said nothing of this. Instead I said, 'That's terrible, and I feel so sorry for Gus. But . . . ' Then I stopped. The sad fact that Rob's father was missing had nothing to do with me. I felt I shouldn't mention it. But something — a streak of curiosity, I suppose — forced me to ask, 'I understand the problem, but how does it affect you, Rob?'

He stared straight ahead, and I understood he was sorting out emotions, and then words. Half-turning, he looked into my eyes. 'Goldie . . . it's something I find hard to talk about. Of course losing my father bothers me. And the ongoing court case about the inheritance is the reason why I can't afford to buy my own transport; why I lived in that awful old house in Torquay, and now why I'm shacking up with Uncle Gus.'

We were silent for a long moment, until he said with an ironic chuckle, 'I'm unemployed, so I have no money coming in; and until I know about the inheritance, I can't really look for a permanent job.' He turned and smiled faintly at me. 'I do some work with Donna at the gallery, but it doesn't earn me much.'

Donna at the gallery. I blinked away uneasy thoughts and said vaguely, 'But the photography — don't you earn anything with that? I mean, your work is excellent.'

His smile had gone, and his voice was rough. 'I'm just one of many people trying to catch the one photo that hopefully will bring in the money. But I haven't found it yet.'

What could I say? We didn't know each other well enough for me to offer comfort or even understanding. So I said the next thing that came into mind. 'Why don't we go and have a coffee somewhere, Rob? There's a great little café near here.' I got up and he did so, too; but I saw from his expression that talking about his problem was a growing concern for him.

The gardens were shadowy now as the sun slowly disappeared behind the dividing wall that led into Northernhay. We walked in silence, but I had a feeling that just talking to me had helped Rob in some small way.

Over coffee, he smiled at me and said teasingly, 'Are you by way of being an agony aunt? Sorry if I talked too much.'

I shook my head and stirred my coffee. 'Please don't apologise. After all, that's what friends are for, isn't it? To listen, and help each other if they can.'

His eyes were dark, and I wondered if my simple words had been too much for him.

'Friends,' he said. 'Yes, you're right, Goldie. Can I reckon you to be one of them? A new friend who listens quietly while I go on and on?'

The smile was back, and I felt relief pound through me. His friend. I finished my coffee and said briskly, 'Of course you can, Rob.' Then I knew I had to stop this emotional conversation before I got too involved. I stood up and said unsteadily, 'I have to go. Perhaps we can meet up again soon?'

For a moment he just sat and looked at me with sea-dark eyes. Then he rose, nodded, and said with a note of resignation in his deep voice, 'Of course. I'd like to call on your aunt this week. Could we go together, do you think?'

Suddenly my heart rose, and I smiled at him. 'That would be lovely. How about Thursday afternoon? Three o'clock?'

'Great. Well, cheers, Goldie. Until we meet again.'

As I walked back to the car park, I thought he had lost some of that unhappiness that had so upset me. And then my mind flew back to earth. Could I make Nick understand that I needed Thursday afternoon off work?

6

As I had feared, Nick was not pleased at the idea of giving me an afternoon off. He looked at me with a frown, drawing down his dark eyebrows like the devil himself.

'What's all this about? First of all an afternoon visiting your aunt, what, last week? And then yesterday, saying you had to fit something in between two important business calls.' The frown darkened. 'Did you do it? I haven't had your report yet.'

'I'm printing it out right now, Nick. I'll put it on your desk as soon as it's done.' We stared at each other, and I saw the forceful expression on his face lighten a bit. I widened my smile and said sweetly, 'So is it all right about Thursday afternoon?' I paused, picked up my phone and put it into my bag, then jangled the car keys to show him I was fully prepared for work. But not on Thursday afternoon.

He shook his head, looked at me with an even harder expression, and then suddenly looked back as he turned away, returning to his own office. Over his shoulder, he said grumpily, 'OK, Goldie. Have your Thursday afternoon. But don't keep asking for more. And be prepared to tell me why you need all this time off. I don't like my staff playing games with me.' His phone rang and he disappeared, shutting the door behind him.

I sighed with relief, then took the report out of the printer and prepared to take it to him, thinking that since he was on the phone, I wouldn't have to say any more. But he put down the phone as I entered his office, sat back in his chair, and grinned at me.

'Goldie, I've asked you before, but this time I hope you'll change your mind. Come out for dinner, won't you?'

I put down the report and stared, confusion filling me. Would I get the sack if I said no again?

His eyes, deep blue with heavy lashes, stared back, and then a smile lit his face. 'You can say where and when. Don't keep me at such a distance — I'm fond of you, you know.'

Yes, I did know. It had grown obvious the longer we worked together. 'Thanks, Nick,' I said. 'I'd like to come out with you. But . . . ' I stopped, unsure how my next words might be received. ' . . . just as friends. Understood?'

He picked up the report, eyes skimming the first page. Then he looked up at me. The smile had gone and the deep blue eyes were narrow. 'Of course, Goldie.'

The report dropped back onto the desk and I turned to go, hoping the expression on my face didn't upset him further. 'Thanks, Nick,' I said in a businesslike voice. 'How about the Midnight Bar in Gandi Street? It has a good reputation. About sevenish tonight? See you then?'

His final words followed me back into my own, smaller office. 'I'll pick you up. Just to make sure you don't change your mind and walk out on me.'

I felt irritation mingle with growing anger, but was sensible enough to know that one didn't really quarrel with one's boss. Not if you wanted to keep your job, which I did. So I pushed away the annoyance. 'I'll be there, Nick. And thanks.'

I sat down, looked at the details of the next job, which would take me back into Cornwall tomorrow, and then found myself wishing dinner tonight could be with Rob — certainly not with Nick.

He arrived on the dot, his open car gleaming in the late-afternoon sun. He smiled, opened the door for me, and then leaned in, saying with a charm he rarely showed, 'I'm glad you're here, Goldie. I know I'm a bit of a brute sometimes, but this evening I'll be as sweet as honey. OK?'

I nodded, rather amused by his own

self-description. When he started driving to the nearest car park, I said calmly, 'I don't think you're a brute, Nick. Just someone who wants his own way.'

We laughed then, and I felt something had warmed between us. *Friendship*, suggested my mind, and I nodded to myself, but also resolved that it would never become more. And then I had an uncomfortable thought that perhaps *he* expected more.

The Italian café was quiet, and we sat in a small alcove, looking out into the street. The fragrance of flowers mingled with the cooking smells of garlic and herbs from the kitchen at the back of the bar.

Nick looked at the menu and then at me. 'Pasta, Goldie? And something exciting with it?'

'I leave it to you, Nick. I'm really only interested in plain food, but I'll give something different a go.'

He nodded, smiled, and ordered some white wine from the hovering waiter. Then he looked at me with a businesslike expression. 'Well,' he said, 'tell me what's going on in your life that's so much more important than doing your work properly?'

The pasta dish arrived, and this gave me a few minutes to concoct a responsible answer. Of course I couldn't tell him about Rob and the bird photographs. But I supposed, fork posed to taste the wonderful-looking plate in front of me, I could tell him about Aunt Mary. That should keep him quiet, surely.

We raised our glasses, and I thought he looked more human than I'd seen him before; and so instead of going on about Aunt Mary, I suddenly decided to tell him about Gus and his childhood at Cliff House. I said, 'I met this man, this painter, called Augustus Grayling. He likes everybody to call him Gus.'

Nick raised a querulous eyebrow. 'And?' he asked drily.

'He used to live at Cliff House, you

know at St Methyr, the one we've recently let out. And I have a bit of a worry that the present visitors won't respect the place properly.'

Our glasses were refilled. 'Does this Gus man know that we're dealing with the contract for Cliff House?'

I recognised the harsher voice and looked down at my plate. 'No; I didn't tell him. I thought I might just drop in there and ask the caretaker if everything is OK.'

Nick's hand reached across the table and took mine away from my plate. I looked at him, not knowing what to expect; but he had a slight smile on his face, and his voice was quiet. 'You're a proper softie, Goldie, when it comes to hard-life stories. I mean, what if the visitors *have* made a mess of the place? He doesn't live there anymore. If there's anything wrong at the close of the contract, we'll sue them and get a payback for repairs. I don't understand why you're worried about this man.' The smile switched to a quick grin.

'Not a new boyfriend, is he?'

I nearly dropped my fork. 'No,' I said quickly and sharply. 'He's old and he's a good artist, and his nephew who lives with him told me that he spends a lot of time reliving his childhood memories. So you see — '

'I think I do see,' said Nick with a frown. 'It's the nephew you're involved with, and he'll be pleased if you do something for his poor old uncle. Is that it?'

'No,' I snapped. 'Nothing to do with his nephew. I just want to be sure that — '

'To be sure that the nephew thinks you're a good girl and deserves to have a kiss and hug.' He pushed his half-empty plate away and glared at me. 'Time you got your feet on the ground, Goldie, and no more of this drifting away in fairy stories.'

That did it; I'd had enough. I got up, found my jacket and draped it round my shoulders, then turned to face him. He was looking at me in astonishment, but I knew I had the upper hand right now. I said calmly, and with a smile that meant nothing, 'Thank you, Nick, for asking me out to dinner. But if I'd had any sense I would have said no; and as it is, there's only one thing I can do. I'm going. Goodbye.'

At the door I was pretty sure he would come after me to say sorry, and we would become friends again. But he hadn't moved. He simply sat at the table drinking wine, and the expression on his face told me that I was wrong. Nick was sure he was right, and he thought of me as a fantasy creature, always feeling sorry for people. Well, I didn't feel sorry for anyone but myself at that moment.

I drove home and sat down with a strong coffee and thought about tomorrow, which I knew would be difficult, even disastrous.

But in the morning I had different thoughts. Yes, perhaps he was right, and I was a sucker for a sad story. But I was also good at my job. And in a way, I respected Nick for being honest with me.

I arrived early, hoping to make a good impression. And then, surprise, surprise, on my desk lay a beautiful bunch of creamy white roses. The fragrance was wonderful, and I could feel my annoyance fading away. There was a note in the wrappings. It said, *Take what time you want, Goldie, but please don't leave. Sorry about last night. Can we do it again sometime? Nick.*

I sat there for what seemed a long time, until I heard Nick in his office talking on the phone. When he'd finished, I made up my mind and slowly went towards his half-open door, knocked and went in. Our eyes met, and he was the first to speak. He stood up, came around his desk and stood close to me.

'A new day,' he said, a smile lighting his face and bringing a shine to those dark eyes. 'I've said I'm sorry, Goldie.'

'Thank you, Nick. Well, we know

where we stand now, don't we?'

He nodded and touched my arm. 'You're right. I'm the boss, but you must have time to live your own life.' He grinned. 'Your soft, sentimental life, Goldie, which is something I admire.'

We looked deeply into each other's eyes, and then I said with a warm smile, 'I'm glad we're friends again. I'll take an hour off today, this afternoon, to step into my fairy-tale world. And thanks, Nick, for those beautiful roses. The scent will stay with me all day.'

He nodded, returned to his desk and then watched me leave the room, smiling with satisfaction.

The morning passed quickly, and I finished several reports of holiday lets which I knew would keep Nick happy while I was away in the afternoon. I attended a sandwich sitting in Rougemont Gardens, wondering where Rob was, and then was off to Cornwall. The sun shone, my business in St Austell only took half an hour, and then I headed for St Methyr and the house on the cliff.

As I drove, I thought about Gus and his childhood at Cliff House. I wondered if he would ever want to go back there — and then I started planning how to get him there. But no clever scheme presented itself, and then I was knocking on Flo's cottage door and feeling the sea breeze playing with my hair.

She opened the door, and her smile widened as she said warmly, 'Why, 'tis Miss Smith. Come in! I've just put the kettle on.'

I thought how lovely it was here; not just her old neat-as-a-pin cottage, but here in Cornwall, which had always held the key to my heart. A she handed me a mug of strong tea and offered newly made scones, I thought back to Nick's scornful words about being a softie and nodded to myself. Yes, I was. I cared for people and wanted their lives to be all they dreamed for themselves. And if that was a fairy tale, then Nick had a lot to learn.

Flo was looking at me from her old chair across the hearth. 'Something wrong?' she asked, and I snapped out of my thoughts and smiled back at her.

'No, not a thing, Flo. Just called in to see how things were going with the holidaymakers. No complaints, I hope?'

'They're having a lovely time, they tell me. They're on the beach most days — and they love the old house, too. They keep asking about who lived here long ago.'

I sipped my tea. 'Could you tell them that?'

'Why yes. I'm getting old, but my memory is still good. That artist who lived here as a child — everyone called him Gus.' She looked into the distance and then back at me, and her voice grew soft. 'Poor boy he was then. Something bad had happened in the family and he never got over it. I liked him and did what I could to make him happier.'

Something told me this was an

important moment. I leaned closer to her. 'What was that sad thing, Flo?'

She gave me her full attention, and I saw the smile droop a little, just as her voice did. 'One of the girls living here, oh, long ago, was unmarried but had a child. Gus was the son of that child, so I believe. He was always worried about finding his father.' The smile returned. 'Let me fill your cup?'

7

Thursday afternoon I was with Aunt Mary good and early. She looked a bit pale, I thought, and I wondered if Rob and I would be welcome. But she smiled and told me to sit down, and then asked — and I thought her voice was weak today, 'What have you been doing, Marigold? Working hard, I expect.'

'This and that,' I told her quietly. 'Yes, work, of course; but work gave me an enjoyable visit to Cornwall last week. And it was a beautiful day — somehow sun and sea came together.'

We looked at each other, and I saw her eyes grow dim as if she were back in the past. 'Ah yes,' she murmured. 'Cornwall, and those lovely days.'

There was a knock at the door, and Rob appeared. I thought how polite and charming he was as he took Aunt

Mary's hand and smiled at her. 'It was good of you to let me come again, Mrs Seaton. We won't tire you with a long visit, will we, Goldie?' He pulled up a chair and sat beside me.

I felt bathed in a lovely warm light — he had called me Goldie again! Somehow I managed to remember why we were here and said to Aunt Mary, 'I think Rob would like to know what you think of his photograph of the Crosby girls, Aunt.'

She nodded, and I watched her thin lips set a little more tightly. I wondered if we were pushing her into memories she would rather forget, but after a pause she smiled at us both, sat up a little straighter, and said firmly, 'It really is a beautiful photograph, Mr Tyson.'

He said quickly, 'Rob, please.'

She smiled more freely at him. 'Very well, Rob. I know how it's shortened names everywhere now.' She waited for a moment and then said with amusement in her voice, 'Not like those

Crosby girls. Always stayed with the names they were christened with — Edwina, Rose and Harriet.' She frowned. 'But, of course, I suppose Rose is a shortened version of Rosalynd — or even Rosetta.'

'Or Rosemary,' I suggested.

She sighed a great gust of air that seemed to leave her exhausted.

'Aunt Mary,' I asked anxiously, 'are you all right?'

Rob stood up and took a step nearer her chair. 'A glass of water, perhaps? Shall I go downstairs and get one?'

And then as if by magic, she was herself again, looking at us with amusement in her faded eyes and gesturing for us both to sit down. 'Talking about names has made me realise that old tales, both funny and sad, are better if they're talked about. So let me tell you about Rose.'

We sat down again and looked at her expectantly.

'I've already told you the girls' father was strict indeed, and all he wanted for them was a good marriage to a kindly man — one who had enough money to keep them in the way they were used to.'

I nodded encouragingly. 'But one of them disobeyed her father, Aunt — you told us about Edwina becoming a VAD in the war.'

'Yes,' she agreed, and then smiled more fully. 'But Colonel Crosby was a military man, you see, so he approved of his eldest daughter going into the nursing profession. But Rose — oh dear me, what a sorry tale.'

I heard her breath rise and fall faster than I liked. I gave Rob a glance and we both stood up. I took one cold hand and rubbed it, and Rob bent over her, saying quietly, 'Shall I get someone to come up to you, Mrs Seaton? You don't look well.'

Aunt Mary took a huge breath and straightened up from her stooping posture. I met her eyes and saw great determination in them. Her voice, when she spoke after a moment's pause, was brisk and far more audible. 'Sit down,' she ordered, and a smile lifted her face. 'Just old age, my dears. Wait till it's your turn! But where was I? Ah yes, just going to tell you about Rose.' She directed her smile towards Rob. 'A glass of water would be helpful, thank you, Rob. I'll wait till you come back to tell you this horror story.'

Rob glanced at me before he left the room, and I said to Aunt Mary, 'I can't believe one of those lovely girls was part of a horror story, Aunt — do go on.'

She lifted her head a little higher and the smile broadened out. 'Neither did I, when I heard about it! But life is full of odd people and odd lives, isn't it?'

I nodded and waited. But then Rob was back, with Matron going straight to Aunt Mary and saying firmly, 'I think you've had enough for the afternoon, Mrs Seaton. I've brought you a nice drink, and I suggest you have a little sleep before tea. Are you comfy and warm enough in that chair?'

'Yes, thank you, Matron. Ah yes, I

feel a little nap would be welcome.'

Matron looked at Rob and me. 'Enough,' she said quietly. 'Give her a chance to recover her thoughts. It must be hard, with nearly a hundred years' worth of memories, to relive some of them. I suggest you come again another day.'

Of course we agreed, and both of us said quiet goodbyes to Aunt Mary, who looked half-asleep already. We followed Matron out of the room, and as we walked downstairs, she said, 'She does so well, but I think too much excitement is bad for her. So many memories, and no doubt some of them unhappy ones.' She smiled. 'Come again, Ms Smith and Mr Tyson — just give her a day or two to recover.'

Outside, we went to our separate cars. Rob, I noticed, had an old Vauxhall that had seen better days. But he merely grinned when I said, 'That's a good old one — goes well, does it?'

He nodded his head and his smile was friendly. 'On loan from Gus — my birthday's in a day or so, and he said I should use this one until I could buy a new one. He's a good man, is my uncle.'

I was about to say splendid, and then something struck me. His birthday! Surely he and I could celebrate somehow? As he watched me open my car door, I looked back and said, 'I have to go down to Cornwall again next week. Fancy a day out?'

He said nothing for a long moment, and I imagined him thinking whether he should say yes or not. Then smiled. 'Sounds good. I'll take my camera. Who knows? I might find the right subject for that competition. Which day, Goldie? What time, and should I come and pick you up for a change?'

I thought quickly. What if Nick saw him park this old car and then come in and collect me? I didn't want any more of that critical, even if only teasing, talk about Rob being my boyfriend. So I called back hastily before I could change my mind, 'Rob, I'm busy in a couple of houses in Exeter on Monday — but I could be at Castle Court about lunchtime. OK with you?'

'Sure. See you then. Cheers, Goldie.'

I watched him drive off and kept my fingers crossed that the old Vauxhall would take him home safely. As I drove towards Torquay and my lonely little flat, I wondered if I had done the right thing. It was clear that Rob was a man on a mission — to find a new life, to win a competition, to help old Gus in what small ways he could. So should I throw myself at him like this?

But by the time I was home, I had made a plan I knew I wouldn't change. When I picked him up next Monday I would have a picnic basket in the back of the car. We would drive out of the city and find a quiet country spot where we could sit, eat and chat. And then I would take him into Cornwall, to Cliff House, where I must tell him that Gus once lived there, and what did he think about that?

Late that evening I remembered that

Donna from the gallery was going to see Aunt Mary with me. I didn't want her to come. I had a feeling that, in spite of her petite size and ready smile, she was a tough businessperson who planned how to get all she wanted — and then got it.

I phoned her before I went to bed because I didn't want to have bad dreams about her bothering Aunt Mary. I told her briefly that my aunt was unwell, and we must cancel our visit. I said I would contact her when Aunt had improved She sounded disappointed and a bit sharp.

'Oh dear, I do hope she'll soon be better. It's so important to get what background we can, ready for the exhibition.' She paused. 'Let me know when we can visit again, will you, Ms Smith — oh, er, Goldie, isn't it?'

I snapped back, 'It may be some time, but yes, I'll contact you. Goodbye now, Miss Adams — oh, er, Donna.'

Anger rose in me, because I was becoming increasingly sure that having to think back over almost a hundred years was making poor Aunt Mary feel strained and possibly unhappy. And I couldn't let that happen. This wretched Donna obviously had no compassion for a hundred-year-old. I would think twice about telling her anything in future, I decided, and felt all the better for the decision.

At the office, Nick was watching me closely, either from inside or poking his head into my room. At one point he came over to my desk and said, 'OK, Goldie? Roses still alive, then?' His smile was a mixture of hope and charm; and despite being so annoying and interrupting my work, I felt a bit sorry for him.

I smiled. 'They're still lovely, Nick.' I looked pointedly at my computer and then back at him. 'Er, anything else?'

He shrugged his heavy shoulders and took a step away. 'No, nothing new. Just keep up the good work — like I know you will.' He nodded and then went back to his own office.

I felt mean. Nick was a good man, and clearly he fancied me. How sad, I thought, that I couldn't return the feeling. What had he said recently? That I was too soft, and should keep my feet on the ground? I closed the file I was working on, sat back and decided to have an early night. My work was up to date, and I had dealt with the contract and papers for tomorrow, so why shouldn't I go home half an hour earlier than usual? I left the office, slipping past Nick's door, hoping he wouldn't notice. He didn't, too busy shouting at someone down his phone.

The afternoon was sheer beauty: sunshine to gloat over and birds singing in the trees of the gardens as I walked through them half an hour later. Slowly I began to understand where my feelings were centred. Nick was my friend; and Rob — ? I thought it over until the peace of the gardens calmed me down as I sat on one of the benches. Eventually I began to realise which of the two I could so easily love.

But I left it there, because a huge decision like that must have time to balance itself. I visited Aunt Mary a few days later, after ringing Matron and asking if it was sensible to visit now.

She answered quickly and firmly, 'Yes, please come — I'm sure your aunt would like to see you. But no more memories, please — you see, someone came yesterday after tea and tired Mrs Seaton out with so many questions. I had to ask her to leave. After all, your aunt is a great age, and we mustn't run the risk of her falling ill before the famous hundredth birthday. So yes, please come, but don't overtire her.'

I said I agreed completely, and would only chat to Aunt Mary without going back into the past. But before Matron said goodbye, I asked a question to which I thought I knew the answer already. 'Who was the visitor, Matron? A Miss Donna Adams, perhaps?'

'I forget the name, but she said she'd come from the gallery in Exeter. Anything else, Ms Smith?'

'No, thank you, Matron. I'll come in for a few minutes after tea — is that all right?'

'Of course. I know Mrs Seaton will be glad to see you.'

I went out to my car and sat there for a short while, thinking about the selfishness and lack of compassion of Donna Adams, and what I would say to her next time we met.

8

As I drove away, some of Aunt Mary's words came back to me. *A horror story — about Rose.* I almost missed a traffic light, so loud were the words running around my head; and when I got home I sat down at once and simply thought.

War time and horror all around, yes, I could understand that. But what could sweet-looking Rose have possibly done to add to that horror? It must have been shocking to make poor Aunt Mary weak at the knees, remembering. Ah well, I told myself, she would eventually tell me, and then we could forget all about it. And in the meantime, I must think about the picnic lunch I planned for Sunday, when Rob and I would drive down to Cornwall and St Methyr.

Sunday opened out into a beautiful day after a misty start. I felt excited, as if I were a child again, looking forward to a day's outing. As I packed the picnic basket and then took a long look at myself in the mirror, wondering if glowing cheeks and sparkling eyes meant what I was feeling, I suddenly had a new thought. I was on the way to falling in love again. Mark's betrayal of our relationship had at last faded, and I knew I could look forward to the future. And the future was centred on Rob. No doubt of it. Something warm and thrilling filled me as I drove into Castle Court, parked and then knocked at the door of The Studio.

My smile disappeared as Gus opened the door and stared at me. 'Well, all ready to go out and have a good day? Too bad it won't happen.'

I nodded, feeling disappointment rising inside of me. What did he mean, it wouldn't happen? Of course it would. The picnic was packed, I looked good in my jeans and new top, and the sun shone. Flatly, I asked, 'Why won't it happen? Where's Rob? I thought he'd be ready. I mean, we said ten o'clock, and I just heard the church clock ring as I drove past. Where is he?'

Gus smiled, stepped back and said gently, 'Come in and I'll tell you all about it.' I followed him into the kitchen, untidy as I remembered, but with a kettle humming and mugs laid out on the table. 'Sit you down,' said Gus, 'and we'll have a nice mug of coffee. That'll cheer you up. And — see here — he left you a note.'

I collapsed into a chair and picked up the small card he handed me. Rob's business card, with the small bird in the corner, and a message on the back. Taking a deep breath, I read what he had written.

Goldie, sorry, but a rare bird has been blown off course in Norfolk and I have to go and see it and photograph it. Will contact you when I get back. Sorry about the picnic. R. And there it ended, just an untidy scrawl filling the back of the card.

I put it on the table, reading it again,

unable to think straight. Gus pushed a mug of coffee under my nose and sat down opposite me. His eyes were gentle and he ran his large hands through the greying hair that needed cutting. 'Well?' he said. 'Cheer up. Worse misfortunes at sea, you know.'

He had a kind voice, and a feeling of warmth pushed across to me. I looked at him, sighed, and realised that Uncle Gus was a good man, despite his rough appearance and slightly eccentric manner. He took a sip of coffee and looked at me across the rim of the mug. 'Where were you going? Somewhere handsome? Nice day, too. Never mind, the lad'll go with you another day.' His grin spread over his face and his voice held amusement. 'Blooming birds, all he thinks about. And just when he could be having a lovely day with you. Well, I know which I'd choose to do in such a case. Birds? No thanks. But a nice day out — that's more like it.' He laughed and grinned at me so that my disappointment began to fade.

I drank my coffee, thinking, and finally realising that if I wanted to be friends with Rob, I had to accept his passion for birds. That made me smile, and then I allowed myself to laugh quietly.

'That's better,' said Gus approvingly. 'You're a sensible young woman. Where were you going for this picnic, then?'

I pushed my empty mug across the table and said with a wry smile, 'Cornwall. A place I love visiting, and I thought how Rob would enjoy it, too.' Then I stopped. I knew what I was going to say next, and wondered what answer this surprising question would bring. 'I know you love Cornwall, Gus — so why don't we go there together?'

He looked at me directly, his eyes full of thoughts under those bushy brows. 'Well . . . '

I wondered if I'd said the wrong thing. What, inviting an elderly man for a pleasant outing? Nothing wrong about that. I gave him a bright, encouraging smile. 'I know Cornwall means a lot to you; it's obvious from those pictures of yours.'

He nodded, and I watched the light fade from his eyes. He cleared his throat. 'Don't know as how I want to go back there, though. Memories, you see. Not always good to return to much-loved places, is it?'

Then I remembered Flo telling me how the small boy had spent many years there, how happy he had been, and I knew at once that this was Gus. She'd told me his name, hadn't she? I'd forgotten the connection, but knew now exactly what I must do: take him back to where he'd been happy. Surely that was the right thing to do?

I stood and grinned down at him. 'Come on, Gus. Get your jacket and we'll go.'

For a stretching moment he looked at me. Then, slowly, he got to his feet and left the kitchen, saying as he went, 'Time to comb my hair and pick up my sketchbook. And then I'll be ready for the adventure.'

I sighed with relief, for the smile he gave me had been a happy one. And the fact that he thought of our day out together as an adventure was great. I knew we could talk as I drove, and perhaps some of the cobwebs of his — and Rob's — past might be revealed. I shouldered my bag and walked to the closed front door, which I opened, and looked out at the big wall behind which Rougement Gardens lay. They would be glorious on this sunny, warm day, and thoughts of Rob suddenly filled my mind. Photographing rare birds! Yes, of course, just the sort of thing he had to do while I took his uncle for a drive in the country. I found myself almost laughing, and realised the shock of not seeing him had disappeared. There would be another day, another picnic, definitely another time for us to be together. My smile grew, and I gladly took the tweed-covered arm that Gus offered me as we left The Studio and headed for my car.

We drove in silence through the busy roads out of Exeter, and I wondered how I would introduce the fact of Gus having lived at Cliff House. But as we drew nearer to Cornwall and at last went over the River Tamar, he seemed to relax in his seat, and glanced at me with a smile. 'I lived here as a child,' he said, and I heard the easiness in his usually hoarse voice.

'Did you?' I thought it better to pretend I didn't know anything about his past. So I just waited for him to talk, if he wanted to.

'Wonderful place. Magical. When I was a boy, I thought it was full of giants and rocky castles.' He sighed. 'Still do. But I don't come like I used to.' He turned, and his eyes fixed on mine. 'Brought up in this wonderful land, I was. Spent most of my childhood here. See, my mother went off and married again, and so Aunt Harriet looked after me.'

I drove a little slower. Now the past

was revealing itself. 'Your Aunt Harriet was one of the Crosby girls, wasn't she, Gus? One of those girls in the portrait by Charles Mason?'

His smile faded. He frowned at me. 'How do you know that?'

'Because my Aunt Mary knew the family, and has told me a little bit about them.'

He was silent, and quickly glancing at him, I saw how he concentrated on the road ahead; but I knew he was full of memories, and I hoped they were all happy ones. Suddenly he came to life again.

'And your Aunt Mary was in love with the artist, Charles Mason. But he went off and so she married a businessman, Tom Seaton, if I recall rightly. Well, how is she? Must be getting on a bit now.'

'Yes, Gus. She has a hundredth birthday coming up in a few weeks. And she's very much alive, but of course she gets tired easily.'

He gave a great noisy laugh that

made me smile. 'Well, wouldn't you get tired if you were that old?'

I nodded my head. 'I get tired out and I'm only twenty-nine. Businesses demand so much of their staff these days.'

His look was long and curious, and as I stopped at a junction, he said quietly but with amusement in his voice, 'Sounds like you'd be better off doing something else. Like following birds about the country, eh?'

I blushed. Really, this was too much. What did he know about Rob and me? But then I understood he was a wise old man who watched people all the time. So instead of snapping back with something like *mind your own business*, I said, 'You're probably right, Gus. I'll think about that as the days go by.'

We drove on without any more talk, and slowly his words began to fill my mind. Was that what I really wanted to do? Leave Nick and my little flat and just follow Rob around the country as he searched for something to win the upcoming competition? It was a decision I was in no state to make, so I said brightly, 'Now I'll tell you where I'm taking you, Gus. We turn right here, down towards the sea.'

He gave a sigh and said, 'To the sea,' and I heard a new note of contentment in his normally rough voice.

Almost before I knew it, we were on the minor road leading to St Methyr. I wondered if Gus was recognising any familiar landmarks, but he sat there in silence, just taking in the beauty of the old road with its enclosing green-laden trees and the occasional glance of the sea below shifting through the leaves. Then I started worrying, when we took the last turn and were in sight of Cliff House, how he would feel. What would he say? Was I right in bringing him here? I knew Rob would have loved it all; but Gus, older and wiser, and with many memories, some of which must be sad?

I stopped in the little parking place

just outside the drive up to the house, sat back, and at last dared to look at him. He said nothing, but I could see his face expressed a mixture of pleasure and pain. I knew I must say something.

'I thought we'd have our picnic on the beach, Gus — but I knew you'd like to see your old home first.'

He sighed and then turned to look at me. A faint smile broke the tautness of his expression. 'Crafty little lady, aren't you, young Goldie? Bringing me here and not saying a word. Afraid of what I might say in return, I suppose. Well, all I can say is thank you. It's wonderful to be home again.'

I explained that the house was let to holidaymakers and that it was occupied at the moment. But Flo, the caretaker, would probably be happy for us to look around the grounds.

'Flo?' he asked as we got out of the car. 'Not Flo who let me play with her own children when things got bad in the house? A lovely lady, as I remember.'

'That's her,' I said brightly. 'She's a bit older now, but she remembered you. And I daresay she'd have the kettle on.'

'Let's see,' he said simply, and we walked slowly up the grass-lined drive to Cliff House.

9

We found Flo putting her washing out on a line across the bottom of her garden.

'Oh, visitors,' she said with a twinkle in her eyes. 'How nice to see you again — Miss Smith, isn't it?'

Gus got there before I could say a word. 'Goldie,' he said. 'And I'm Gus, and you're Flo Bailey. I remember you from the days when I lived here, growing up.' He stood there, looking out over the washing to the sea, and his smile was one I hadn't seen before.

'Well,' said Flo, hurriedly pulling up the line and then turning back to the cottage, 'yes, you're Mr Grayling, and I'm so glad to see you again. Come in — and we'll have something to celebrate, shall we?'

Indoors she bustled about, putting glasses on the table, nodding to us to sit down, and then producing a tall jug of something from the larder. 'Cowslip wine,' she said proudly, pouring us a glassful each. 'They grow on the cliffs, and I make this every year.'

Gus sniffed delicately at the golden liquid, then held up his glass and beamed at Flo. 'We've got quite a few memories of the old days, haven't we, my lover?'

Flo grinned back at him, sipping her wine. 'That's what you did call me! And I used to call you my 'andsome. Remember, do you?'

Gus nodded, and his smile faded. 'I remember more than that, Flo. All about Aunt Harriet bringing me here for the summer holidays. Then she went back to the farm, and I used to wander around on the beach and the cliffs, thinking of my mother and where she'd gone without me.'

'Yes, your mother, Rose. Dearie me, such a sad story.' Flo's wide smile gave way to an expression of sympathy, and I felt myself wonder if this was the horror story Aunt Mary had warned me about.

She put her glass on the table and looked intently at Gus. 'Going off like that . . . well, terrible. And that man, Paul. Not the sort of person she should love, we all thought.'

There was silence for a long moment, and I wondered if should interrupt and ask questions. Then Gus sighed, nodded at Flo, and said, 'But he had a voice like no one else. Taught Rose to sing and then ran off with her.'

Flo studied her glass before saying, 'What I heard was that she ran off with him! Eloped, didn't they? Ran out of the house at midnight and went off to sing together on the stage.'

This was amazing, and not what I had expected of any of the Crosby girls. No wonder Aunt Mary, with her old-fashioned ideas, had thought of it as a horror story. I said quietly, hardly liking to break into this fascinating conversation, 'It must have been war-time — so where did they go to sing?'

Gus took up the family story.

'ENSA,' he said wryly. 'Entertainments National Service Association, formed to take entertainment to armed forces overseas. Oh yes, my mother and Paul were a great success wherever they went. The boys loved them. Beautiful voice she had, and they sang duets, old-time ones. A bit different from the modern tunes of that day, jazz and that stuff. And especially when Rose began to change her style of clothes.' He stopped, looked at Flo, and they exchanged what I read as sly glances of amusement.

I cut in again. 'Why should she do that, Gus? Sounds a bit shocking.' Aunt Mary would definitely have thought so, if the dresses got shorter and the necklines went down. I smiled to myself. How times changed! Understanding the need for entertaining clothes as well as singing and dancing, I said quietly, 'Do go on, Gus. This is becoming an extraordinary story.'

He drained his glass and looked at

me, and I saw deep emotion in his eyes. Slowly he went on. 'Extraordinary? I suppose so, but who knows about people's feelings? Rosetta was the new name she chose, because Rose was so old-fashioned. She and Paul were madly in love, so Rose said when she wrote to her sisters as the war went on. And then . . . well, it happened, just like it does today. She discovered that Paul already had a wife and family in Australia.' He smiled sadly. 'You can imagine what happened when she found out. Trouble! And after a big row, for she was the one of the three sisters with a huge temper, he left her and set sail for home.'

Pausing, he and Flo looked at each other. She put out her hand and he touched it, smiling at her sad face. 'And now we come to the part where things get better.' He looked at me. 'Not bored, are you? Times long ago — what do they mean to you?'

'They mean a lot, Gus. I think you have had a difficult life, or so Rob told me. But please go on. What happened next?'

'I happened!' And suddenly we all laughed, for he grinned, and we felt the sadness was way in the past. 'Yes, Rose was pregnant when Paul went off, and she had me here in the house. But then she went away again.'

'Back to ENSA? Oh, Gus, you mean she left you? So who looked after you?'

Flo spoke up firmly. 'Dear Miss Harriet, who'd married a farmer in Somerset, looked after the poor child. He seldom saw his mother, but we made him as happy as we could when he spent his summer holidays here.'

'You did. I've never forgotten, Flo, how good you were to me. Cared for me. Told me my mum would come back one day.'

She shook her head and looked away from him. 'She never did though, did she? Instead, when the war ended, she came home and married a business-man. Lived in London, they did. And . . . ' She stopped, and I could see

111

her wondering if she should go on. But she did. 'And they had a child; Edmund, who she loved and spoiled to death. Your step-brother, he was. But no, she never came looking for you. Your Aunt Harriet did that.'

Gus nodded his head. 'The farm; I remember it so well. A happy place. But I never forgot Rose. My mother, who abandoned me.'

We all sat there, thinking, and I guessed Gus was feeling this sad story acutely. So I said brightly, in the hope of changing the subject, 'Well, we're going to have a picnic on the beach, Flo, so we'll make a move. Thanks for the wine; it was delicious. Gus, are you ready?' I stood up, looking at him, willing him to say yes. But he shook his head.

'Forget the picnic, my dear. Give me half an hour on my own while I sketch the old house, and then I'll come and find you.'

I nodded. If that was what he wanted, that was OK by me. 'Right,' I said. 'I'll collect a few shells, and then I'll expect you to lunch, Mr Grayling.'

My voice had the desired effect of bringing smiles to the two elderly faces. At the door I turned and smiled at Flo. 'It's been lovely to see you again,' I said quietly. 'I'll be down again before the next lot of holidaymakers come. And Gus — ' I beamed at him. ' — don't forget I'm down there on the beach, will you?'

I saw him put his arms around Flo. They hugged, and I understood the depths of their emotions. Then he found his sketchbook in his pocket, grinned at her, and followed me out of the door. On the way to the beach, as I went down the narrow grassy path towards the golden sands, he turned away, not saying anything, and I knew he was going to sketch his old home.

With sand between my toes and the warmth of the sun on my body freeing those feelings of sympathy for Gus, slowly I walked along, looking down at the tideline for shells. I found a few pretty ones, and then a beautiful polished piece of glass caught my eye. Something mysterious, washed by the ocean into this elegant piece of everyday rubbish I knew I must keep. It was warm and heavy in my pocket, and foolishly I imagined that it was a piece of Cornwall I could treasure, because I knew I would always love this land and sea even though I had to live elsewhere.

Then there was a shout, and Gus was coming down the path, waving at me. Action needed after all that dreaming! I ran back to where I'd left the picnic basket and began spreading the cloth and taking out the food. Smiling at him, I offered a cheese roll, and hoped his sketch would keep him happy when he was back in Exeter.

The day finally ended with a clear sky and the first stars shining. I left Gus at Castle Court, and he kissed me on the forehead before getting out of the car. 'You're a good person,' he said, and I felt proud of doing something that perhaps merited his words. Opening his front door, he turned back and said, 'No sign of the lad. Still off chasing that bird, eh? Never mind. He'll be back sometime.' After a last wave, he disappeared into the house.

I drove away, my mind suddenly overflowing. It had been an emotional visit to Cornwall, and hearing Gus's memories had stirred up my own feelings. I wanted to go home and relax, and think about Rob and his intense passion for photography and birds. I wondered if that passion left any time for thoughts of other people — and even love.

As I carried the basket into the apartment block and up to my flat, I told myself I must stop all this dreaming. Nick's words seemed true. *Too soft. Keep your feet on the ground, Goldie.*

Later, as I drank coffee, the telephone rang. A voice I knew said, 'Goldie?' and my heart beat a little faster. He was back, and ringing me. He sounded as if he had things to talk about. Was I part of that? I wondered.

I crossed my fingers and smiled at the phone until he said firmly, 'I want to see you, Goldie — to talk to you. Can I come around now?'

10

In a flurry of excitement and something like happiness, I scurried around, tidying, fiddling with the flowers in the fireplace and then putting the kettle on. Rob wanted to talk to me! Surely this was what I had wanted all the time — friendly talk between us, opening up, getting to know each other.

When the doorbell sounded, I was there in a second, already smiling, hoping my hair looked all right. 'Rob,' I said, 'how lovely to see you. How was Norfolk? Did you find the rare bird and photograph it?' I led him into the kitchen and then turned, looking into his eyes, wondering why he hadn't answered me. With a pang of sympathy, I recognised the expression on his face — unsmiling, angry with life for treating him badly. I said quietly, 'Something wrong? Did the bird fly off before you could get a shot of it?'

Then I wished I hadn't attempted foolish humour. Clearly his problem was worse than that. I made coffee, produced some biscuits, then sat at the table opposite him. For a moment he just sat there in silence, until slowly he came back to the Rob I thought I knew quite well.

'Sorry,' he said, and smiled at me. 'Why on earth should I pass on my nasty mood to you? Goldie, it really is good to see you again. You're like a light at the end of a tunnel.'

I caught my breath. This sounded serious. I said, 'Well, thanks. I've never been called a light before — more often a waving flicker of something in the far distance!'

We smiled at each other and then he put sugar into his coffee and stirred it, still looking at me. His eyes had cleared. His lips had a lift to them. I felt relief surge through me. But clearly there were things to be sorted out. I decided on action. 'So what's on your mind? Thunder and lightning, by the look of things!'

He nodded, managed a hint of that wonderful grin, and said, 'It's nothing really serious — just that every problem, whatever it is, sinks me into the depths. I get so angry. But yes, you're right — the damned bird flew off. Rare, it was. Good to look at, but too many cameras pointing its way and off it went. That was enough to get me started. Then on the way home, all I could think about was this wretched inheritance. If only my father could be found, then everything could be sorted out. I worry about Gus, you see. The wretched money, according to my father's will, says it should be divided between us, but he always says he doesn't want any of it. Which puts me in a difficult situation. He's been so good to me, and I don't want him to go without in his old age. And when we argue, he gets het up, which I don't want, either.' He stared into his half-empty cup.

I said, 'More coffee? Help to get those blues out of your mind.' As I poured it, I gave him a determined smile I hoped would make him realise that life wasn't always that difficult. I felt the atmosphere clear a bit, and then I said, 'You need something to look forward to. How about a birthday party? This coming week, isn't it, Rob? Got any exciting plans?'

The smile faded and his lips tightened. 'Oh yes, something really great — a party Donna's laying on for me. Well thanks, but I'd rather do something else.'

'Do what, Rob?' My voice was quiet, and I met his keen eyes with an easing of my anxiety.

'Well, I had something a little less formal in mind. Like a quiet party between two people, and perhaps a birthday cake. Somewhere out of doors.' He smiled, and this time it looked real.

I felt a shadow fade inside my mind, and I said rather quietly, because I knew what he meant, 'A picnic, Rob — perhaps on Dartmoor? All that wilderness would be fine for two people.' Dare I ask the all-important question? I took a deep breath. Yes, I dared. 'Just you and me, celebrating your birthday?'

I watched his expression change. The blue mood seemed to have disappeared. Now he reached a hand across the table and touched mine as I put down the coffee cup. 'You and me, Goldie. I've been wanting to say that for ages. So is it all right with you?'

A wave of happiness swept through me, and I pressed his fingers as he held my hand. I beamed at him. 'It's certainly all right, Rob! Let's make a plan, shall we? Day and time? Location? And who's going to make the cake?'

We laughed then, full of relief and happiness, and his hand tightened around mine. It was warm, strong, and exciting. But eventually I knew we must get down to reality again. I slipped my hand out of his and said, 'What's all this about Donna giving you a formal party? In the gallery, of course, it means she'll invite all the important people who help her run it. Would you be allowed to put anything on display?'

He got up, pushed his chair under the table and came around to my side. Strong arms drew me up so that we stood together. The sea-green eyes looked into mine, and his voice was deep and vibrant. 'Yes, she is. All my bird photographs.' He paused. 'Goldie, I have to work for some kind of a living. And if Donna's going to the trouble of setting up a mini-exhibition for me, along with the party, then I can't say no.'

'Of course you can't.' I kept my voice light, but inside I was thinking angry thoughts about Donna. For instance, was the purpose of this party-cum-exhibition because she wanted Rob to thank her, and perhaps slip into a relationship with her to show his gratitude?

I stepped away from him, then

turned. He was watching me, and his smile touched my heart. 'What about your Aunt Mary?' he asked. 'I'd like to see her again. This week, do you think? Early evening when you've finished work?'

I nodded. Things were moving too fast for me to think straight. But a visit to Aunt Mary? Yes, though I would have to calm down before seeing her. And going with Rob would be lovely. 'Yes,' I said, smiling back at him. 'What a good idea. I expect she's getting excited about the birthday celebrations, and she'll want to tell us what's going on.'

We walked to the door, and before he left he looked back at me, saying quietly but with a note of enjoyment, 'And we'll go to Dartmoor for my birthday. Couldn't ask for a nicer present. Not with you there, Goldie.'

Sheer pleasure flooded me, but I had the sense not to give way to it. 'Don't forget the cake!' I said jokingly.

He took a step nearer, then kissed my forehead. 'Aunt Mary, and you, and

Dartmoor — that's really cheered me up. Which evening should we go and see Aunt Mary?'

I felt my breath deepening as I said, 'How about Wednesday? Say six o'clock? And then your birthday on Sunday, when we'll have all day.'

He nodded. 'Quite a plan. Now I must go. See you soon, Goldie.'

Alone again, I returned to the kitchen and sat down, pouring another cup of half-cold coffee, thinking about Sunday, and how it would be between us.

Next morning, in the office, I was caught dreaming at the computer, not reporting on the newest contract for a holiday home, but thinking about Dartmoor. Where exactly would we go? Would Rob enjoy our outing? Would the sun shine? My dreams grew wilder, until Nick came into the room, stood beside me and frowned.

'Goldie, wake up. I need that report, if you could possibly pay attention.'

He sounded exasperated, and really I couldn't blame him. Hurriedly, I picked up the important papers and offered them to him. 'Sorry, I was just about to print it.' I did so, and handed it to him.

He tossed the papers back on the table and walked over to the window. Turning, he fixed me with an angry gaze. 'Look, Goldie . . . get your feet on the ground, won't you?' Then he stopped, and his voice changed as he came closer, beside my chair. 'Why don't you think about getting married? All the practicalities of that would bring you back down to earth.'

'Married?' I blurted. 'What's that supposed to mean? And who should I marry, for heaven's sake?'

There was a slight pause before he said, 'A good respectable chap with a steady job, and perhaps a business that's growing. Someone who can give you a decent home and look after you properly.'

I almost shouted, 'And love me? Any chance of that?'

He put his hand on my shoulder and bent down to me. 'Is that so important,

Goldie? Surely what you really need is someone who can look after you. I mean, love is something that works or doesn't. It's a risk, marrying for love. Think about it.'

I pushed the chair back, shoving him away from me. 'And who is this wonderful guy? Not you by any chance, is it, Nick?'

He scowled. 'That's no way to treat an honest proposal.'

I took in a deep breath and was able to say, more quietly this time, 'Well, thanks for the honour of being proposed to, Nick. But the answer is no.' I walked away and stood with my back to him, wondering if I was now to be treated to an explosion of rage. But it didn't come. Instead, he came over so that we were looking at each other, eye to eye. I saw a sort of smile replace the angry expression that had been there a minute or so ago.

He nodded. 'OK, if that's how you feel.' The smile grew, becoming sly. 'I suppose it's the old guy's nephew, is it?

The man chasing birds? Well, I wish you well with him, Goldie, because he's not what you need.' We still stared at each other. But he hadn't finished. 'And I am. Think about it, will you? And now give me those papers. And may I ask you to stop dreaming and get on with the work?' He left the room without looking at me again, and I was left with my mind in confusion. Did I love Rob? And might he be the one I wanted to marry?

I went home that evening still in a whirl of emotions. After I'd had two cups of strong coffee, I decided to go and visit Aunt Mary. Yes, Rob and I had planned to go on Wednesday, and this was only Monday. But I needed to go. Perhaps listening to her quiet voice would help calm me down. And then, as I changed my clothes and brushed my hair, I had a strange feeling that Aunt Mary needed me more than I needed her. I hurried to Riverside and knocked on the door.

Matron opened it. 'Oh, Ms Smith

— well, I'm afraid your aunt isn't too well. I don't think you should visit her today. Nothing serious, but just old age taking its toll. She'll probably feel much better tomorrow.'

Her smile told me that this was all I needed to know, so I smiled back and said, 'Please give her my love. I'll be here again on Wednesday evening.'

The door closed behind me, and I went home with yet another worry on my mind. How ill was poor Aunt Mary?

11

I rang Riverside the next morning and, thank goodness, Matron said Aunt Mary was feeling much better. 'I think she'd welcome a visit, if you can manage it — today or tomorrow, perhaps?'

'Of course I'll come, Matron, and Mr Tyson will be with me. Please give Aunt Mary my love.'

That cheered me up a lot, and I went to work happily enough, even finding a restrained smile for Nick, who looked up from his desk and seemed to want to say something. An apology, perhaps? But I went straight into my own office and turned the computer on. Feet on the ground — well, really! They were planted strongly today.

I was thinking that it must be lunchtime and I would take a sandwich out into Rougement Gardens, when the phone rang. It was Rob. He sounded quiet, and the words were slow, but I heard every one of them and felt my heart sink almost into my boots.

'Goldie, I've got some good news, and some bad news, too. Which do you want first?'

I heaved a big sigh, but said resignedly, 'Let's have the bad stuff first. And perhaps the good news will make me feel better. So what is it?'

His voice seemed a bit louder, more cheerful. He said, 'I can't keep our date for Wednesday. That's the bad bit. And now . . . well, you see, I've been given a chance to go on a photo gig with a magazine editor who saw one of my bird shots and thinks he'd like me to do some work for him and his paper.' He stopped, and I knew instinctively there was something else.

'And?' I asked.

'My birthday. Our day out on the moor. Goldie, I'll still be away on Sunday. I'm sorry. I was looking forward to it. But perhaps we could catch up when I get back?'

'And when will that be, Rob?' My voice was cold. 'Or are you planning to go off to Antarctica or somewhere before we can have our picnic?'

'Don't be like that. It's not as if I'll be away long. And . . . ' He paused. 'I thought you'd be pleased for me to have some paid work, Goldie. But you don't sound it.'

I sighed again. 'I'm sorry, Rob, and of course I'm thrilled that you've landed a good job. But I was so looking forward to Sunday.'

'So was I. But a few days won't make too much difference, will it? I don't imagine this gig will go on for more than, say, a fortnight. Let's make a date for sometime then, shall we?'

By now I was so sorry for myself that I couldn't control the shake in my voice. I said unsteadily, 'Of course we will. Sorry Rob, but I have to go now. My work, you see.' And I switched off the phone.

Thank goodness for work, I thought,

immersing myself in the latest report waiting to be edited and printed. Once that was done, I realised the morning was over. So — lunch? The sandwich idea seemed good, so I decided to pick one up from the shop on the corner.

As I was about to leave the office, Nick came out and looked at me. He smiled — pleasantly, I thought with surprise. 'Goldie,' he said, 'could we share a lunch? I'd like to talk to you about yesterday. When I was a bit of a brute, I'm afraid.'

I looked at him. Clear eyes, a smile that make him look almost handsome, and a softer note in his usually loud voice. 'OK,' I said. 'I'm going into the gardens with a sandwich. Want to come?'

He raised an eyebrow, but simply nodded. 'Excellent idea. I'll go get the sandwiches, shall I?'

'Chicken and mayo, please, for me. And brown bread.'

Again he nodded, followed me down the stairs and then went off towards the corner shop while I walked into the gardens, found a bench and sat down, immersing myself in this welcome world of lovely flowers and peace. He found me there. I smiled and moved along the bench. 'Good,' I said, 'and we could have a coffee somewhere afterwards.'

'Splendid idea.' He bit into his beef sandwich, swallowed the first mouthful, and then turned to me. 'I really am sorry about yesterday, Goldie. Rather got out of my depth, didn't I?'

I considered, looking at my half-eaten sandwich. 'Well, you asked me to marry you, Nick — was that going out of your depth? And are you here now to say you didn't mean it?'

'No, of course not.' His voice was stronger, and he looked deeply into my eyes. 'You must know that I've always fancied you, Goldie — and it suddenly hit me that I wanted you always with me. As a partner, not just a working colleague.'

His expression was genuine and

almost pleading. I selected the second sandwich and looked at it carefully. Inside me, doubts were coming fast and furiously. Nick had been honest about all this. And although I had turned him down at once, now I realised that he would make a splendid partner, if not a husband. Someone I could rely on. Not just an attractive friend who disappeared into the void whenever some wretched bird arrived on the scene.

Such thoughts, such doubts. I wasn't sure about anything anymore. I said briskly, 'What about that coffee? I'd love one.'

He got up, put the sandwich boxes into a bin, and said, 'I know just the place. Let's go.'

With his hand on my arm, we left the gardens and found an upmarket café near the cathedral. Sitting there among chattering groups of people, I couldn't help thinking that Rob would never have brought me here. He was a picnic man, happy to eat whatever came along, no frills, no nonsense about drinking coffee in a fine china cup — mugs on a kitchen table was what he preferred. I found those thoughts cheering and amusing. And then I decided to bring Nick back to the undoubted knowledge that I was the wrong woman for him. I fumbled in my bag and found my latest treasure — the piece of glass I had found on the beach at St Methyr. I put it on the table, where it caught the brilliant sunlight and shone like a gold piece.

Nick stared, put out his hand and touched it. 'What on earth?' he asked.

'Just a piece of glass I picked up somewhere. It's so beautiful that I carry it about with me, to remind me of a happy day.' I paused. 'It's a sort of charm, I think.'

His eyebrows went up to the roof. 'Goldie, I believe you're telling me that fairy tales are more important than bricks and mortar. Aren't you?'

I smiled, relaxed now, and said quietly, 'If you like to think that, Nick, then you're probably right.' I finished my coffee and got up. 'Back to work. Shall we go?'

The afternoon flashed past, and Nick stayed in his own office. Outside in the sunshine again, I decided to go and see Aunt Mary. Surely she must be feeling better today.

She was. Her smile was bright and happy. 'Oh, Goldie, how lovely to see you. I've got such a lot to tell you. Miss Adams called a few days ago, and well, just sit down and I'll show you.'

I watched her expression. Her face was lit up and enthusiastic, as young as she was at heart. Thank goodness something was going right, I told myself with a wry smile.

'Miss Adams gave me this — isn't it splendid?'

I took it carefully, read the beautifully printed words, and took a deep breath. Donna certainly didn't do things by halves. What must this have cost? I wondered. The message — no, it was an invitation — merely said that the Exeter Gallery for Fine Art hoped that Mrs

Seaton would be able to attend the unveiling of a recently discovered portrait of the Crosby girls by well-known local artist Charles Mason. Two o'clock until three. Tea would be offered. RSVP.

I met her gaze and saw pleasure in it. Of course I would take her. And if Rob was back by then, he would no doubt be there, offering help to Donna. As if she needed any. But such thoughts were unkind and unnecessary. 'Wonderful, Aunt Mary,' I said warmly. 'Shall we write an acceptance? I can do it for you, if you like.'

She was fishing about in the top drawer of the chest near to her, and produced paper and a pen. 'No,' she said firmly. 'I'm not quite in my dotage yet — I'll write it myself.'

'Of course,' I said humbly, and watched while her steady hand wrote down her acceptance of the invitation. 'At least let me post it,' I offered, and she smiled, handed both letter and writing pad to me, and sat back in her chair. She looked tired, I thought, but her smile was alive.

'Miss Adams was pleased to hear more of my tales. She asked what I did in the war, so I had to remember all the goings-on of the WRVS, of which I became the local president.'

I thought, how dare Donna come and worry her like that? But I smiled at Aunt Mary and said quietly, 'I'd love to have seen you, Aunt, in your smart uniform, making jam and joining in singing 'Jerusalem'.'

Her smile faded. 'Goodness me, we didn't just make jam, Goldie. We tinned fruit and vegetables, and oh yes, we were one of the first people to stand up for women's rights, something everybody is on about now. My goodness, I could tell you a few things we did and said.'

We looked at each other, and I saw in her sudden expression what a marvellous woman she must have been in the war. Then she smiled and said, 'I think I've got photographs somewhere of my ladies — my working colleagues. Not sure where, but perhaps in my writing desk. I must look them out.'

I thought at once how pleased Donna would be to be able to show some of Aunt Mary's life as well as the painting of the Crosby girls, and I felt quite angry. I wondered if it was necessary to bring Aunt Mary into this at all, but of course the public must be told where the portrait was at the moment. And then she really surprised me.

'I must have my hair done before we go, and perhaps a new hat? What do you think, Goldie?'

I thought hard. Freshly styled hair perhaps, but no hat. If the public must learn about Aunt Mary, I wanted them to see her just as she was, coming up to a hundred, and still so full of life and love. 'No hat, Aunt,' I said. 'Please just be yourself.'

She smiled at me, but was silent for a few moments until she reached out, took my hand, and said quietly, 'You're a good girl, Goldie. Helpful and loving.

I do so hope that a nice man will find you. You deserve to have a good marriage, you know.'

I swallowed as my emotions arose and swept through me. I nodded at her, unable to find words, and I thought of Rob, imagining him working up there in London and probably forgetting me as the work took over. But then my instinct told me that he wasn't like that; not a man like Nick with no time for thinking, or wondering or imagining.

As I looked into Aunt Mary's watchful eyes, I said something I thought I would never say. My voice was low and a bit unsteady. 'I think I love someone a lot, Aunt. It's wonderful, but it's so difficult. You see, I don't know how he feels about me. Do you think love is always like this?'

She bent her head, and I heard the smallest sigh leave her lips. Then she looked up again, smiled at me, and said, 'Yes, Goldie. Love is hard to chase about, always hoping it will settle down and give you all that you know it offers.'

We nodded at each other, and I felt she was going to add something that might comfort me. 'Yes, I see.' My smile grew. 'Well, that's cheered me up a bit, Aunt. And now I think I ought to go.'

'Stay a little longer, child. I have a story to tell you that might clear your mind a bit.' Her smile faded, and I thought I saw memories in her eyes. 'It's about me,' she said in a low voice, 'and Charles Mason.'

12

I think my mouth dropped open and I felt my eyes widen. Aunt Mary and Charles Mason? But she married Frederick Seaton, so what was this all about? Then, watching her, seeing the far off look in her eyes, and the softening of her lined face, instinctively I knew this was a love affair. She wanted to tell me how it came about and how it ended, for it must have done. And what memories she must be nursing at the back of her mind, even now in extreme old age.

I took her hand. 'I'd love to hear about Charles Mason — how you came to meet him and the rest of it. But only if you really want to tell me, Aunt.'

'I do, yes, I do, Goldie.' For a moment she held my gaze, and then looked up at the portrait of the Crosby girls just behind her. 'You see, we were all so young . . . ' I nodded, and slowly she went on. 'I think I told you that the girls were all musical, and Charles Mason was invited to give them lessons. That was when he painted their portraits. He lived near Cliff House, and worked in his studio there. But as well as his talent for painting, he was a trained concert pianist.' Her voice dropped. 'Such a lovely man. And I had the good fortune to meet him, as my family were friendly with the Crosbys, and I spent time with them on the beach, shopping, or just being at home in that warm, welcoming house. And so you see, I fell in love with this handsome, gifted man, and he with me.'

I thought back into the past. 'But you married Uncle Fredrick — how did that happen?'

She sighed. 'My parents decided he'd make me a good husband. He owned his business and was well off.'

I looked into her eyes and saw the

rest of the story there. 'So Charles Mason — ?'

'Was killed early in the war, soon after D-Day when we invaded France and started liberating Europe. And I was talked into marrying Frederick. I became Mrs Seaton, but I've never forgotten those days we had together, Charles and I.'

A new understanding of life suddenly hit me. One didn't dream forever. Reality often came and demolished those dreams, unless one was lucky. Now I said slowly and with thoughts thronging my mind, 'You're warning me that love doesn't always come as you expect it to.'

She nodded. 'Yes, Goldie. I don't want you to be hurt, but I thought you needed to know that even although love is important — of course it is — friendship can sometimes take its place.'

'You and Uncle Frederick became friends, then?'

'Yes, we did. Fond friends, and I was

144

grateful for that. But I've never forgotten Charles. And that's why it's important to me that his lovely portrait will go on show.'

'Of course — I understand, Aunt. And thank you for helping me to know that life doesn't always turn out as you hoped.'

We smiled at each other, and instinctively I put my arms around her. 'Thank you,' I whispered. I sat back. She looked weary but her eyes were bright. 'I must go now, dear Aunt Mary. And I'll be here to see you again in a few days.'

'Will you bring that nice Mr Tyson — Rob — with you, Goldie? Such a charming young man.'

'Yes, I hope I will. He's away at the moment — but . . . ' Something made me face the truth. ' . . . I think I love him, Aunt.'

'Then you must be ready to wait, if necessary; and if he doesn't love you enough, to let him go.'

She watched me, and I guessed all

my thoughts were there on my face. But I didn't want to leave her without acknowledging all she had told me. I got up and said, 'You've taught me a necessary lesson, Aunt Mary. I'll remember it, and thank you for all the new doors you've opened.'

With a last loving smile, I left her in her quiet room, seeing that as I turned in the doorway she was looking at the portrait on the wall; and I knew that the Crosby girls would be as pleased as she was that Charles Mason was still remembered. And still loved.

On the way home, I decided to call and see that Gus was all right. He came to the door and at once gave me that wry smile. 'Ah, you again. Ready to take flight and chase the young man, are you, Goldie? He won't be back for a while, you know.'

I found a smile. 'Can I come in? I'd love a cup of tea, please, Gus.'

'So he told you about this bit of work, did he? Which might well develop into a proper job if he gets the right shots.' He lifted his eyebrows and stared at me intently. 'Come on in and I'll brew us a pot.'

Entering the kitchen behind him, I caught the look of half-hidden amusement he threw me before switching on the kettle. But with a straight face, he said, 'And if so, ready to fly after him, are you?'

I paused and tried to straighten out my thoughts. Then I said quietly, and I hoped with no sign of the raging emotion inside me, 'No, Gus, I'm not flying after anyone. I believe that people should lead their own lives without any entanglements.'

He put spoonfuls of tea into the brown pot and looked at me again, this time with a serious expression. 'So all this stuff about love in your mind is just a brief few weeks together and then break it off?'

'No,' I said fiercely. 'If I really love someone, I'll give it to him as a present and let him do what he wants.'

Gus poured tea and pushed the milk

bottle across the table. 'Hmm,' he said in his dark, rough voice, 'one in a million you are, Goldie, my girl. Now drink that up, and then I must get back to the daubing.'

'You mean painting,' I said with a big smile.

He shook his head. 'I mean daubing, and you know what I mean. But if it's painting to you, well then, thank you. You're very kind.'

We parted at the open doorway and he nodded at me. 'Come again; you're always welcome. Even if that bird-chasing chap stays away, give him a bit of time. He needs it, you know.' Unexpectedly he stooped and kissed me on both cheeks. 'We all have to live in hope.' We stared at each other, and then he said, 'Off you go,' and shut the door as I walked over the cobbles, back to my car and the lonely drive back to Torquay. And to the lonely flat.

But now I had new thoughts. I telephoned Nick and said quickly, 'I want a favour, Nick. Please listen and don't shout at me.'

'What is it this time? Another afternoon off, I suppose? What do you do with all this time off? Goldie, I do believe you lead a secret life.' Amusement lightened his voice now, and I crossed my fingers, hoping he would agree to my slightly odd suggestion.

'Nick, I'd like you to spend Sunday with me — Dartmoor looks wonderful at this time of year, and I imagine there are many good pubs and restaurants out there where we could have lunch. Could we do that, do you think?'

'Dartmoor? Are you out of your mind?'

'I believe there's one particular place where the chef is famous. Surely you'd like to see how he cooks? I mean, you and your cookery course — I bet you're ready to learn a bit more, aren't you?' I couldn't bear it if he said no. How, otherwise, would I spend Rob's birthday? Alone? Unloved?

'Well . . . ' His voice was quieter, and I imagined his face slowly lifting in an interested smile. 'Where is this wonderful place?'

'Bowden Manor,' I said. 'Just beyond Chagford — not far. And I'm willing to drive.'

'We could take turns; I'd rather do that.'

'All right,' I said. 'At least allow me to drive to Exeter, and then I'll agree to be in the passenger seat of your gleaming monster. Around twelvish, perhaps?'

'Right.' There was a pause, and then he said more gently, 'And clothes? Smart casual would be about right for this famous place, Goldie. And make it pretty, please — I can't stand going out with a woman who has no style.'

'Don't worry, I'll do my best. And if you don't approve, I'll go and buy a sandwich somewhere less particular about clothes.'

He laughed. 'I bet you would, too. No, Goldie, I have faith in your dressing-up ideas.' He paused again. 'But I just don't understand why you're doing this — a date gone wrong, perhaps? Not that bird man, is it?'

My smile died, and my voice was so quiet I wondered if he could hear me. 'Of course not, Nick. Just that — well, I want to repay you for allowing me all the time I've been taking off.' A white lie, but did it matter? At least it would stop him — and me — from thinking any more about Rob. We chatted on for a bit and then I said, 'Sorry, Nick, but I really must go and do a few jobs. See you at the office tomorrow.'

He said, more gently than I ever expected him to sound, 'Lovely to talk to you, Goldie. And it's so nice to think we're growing a bit closer. Well, at least I hope so.'

I felt something uncomfortable inside me and knew it was all my fault for deciding to spend Sunday with him. Did he really think we were getting closer? I knew I wasn't, but I wondered if he was speaking honestly. If so, I had better look out, for Nick Burns had a habit of getting what he wanted. And if that applied to me, than I would have done better to stay at home and think about Rob rather than going out with him, and possibly giving him false ideas about my feelings. But it was done, and I wouldn't humiliate myself by calling it off. Perhaps it would be a pleasant morning and a good lunch. I grinned as I got up, feeling brighter and wondering just what I would wear. Please the hotel and please Nick — well, it was better than being here alone and wondering when Rob would return.

Sunday turned out to be a good summer morning. There was a touch of mist lying about the town, and the lightest breeze to cool things down if they got too hot. My wardrobe offered several possible outfits, but eventually I chose a new white silky ruffle-necked shirt and a pair of light grey well-cut trousers, and around my neck I folded a vivid blue patterned scarf. I took trouble with my hair, even put kohl around my eyes, and then thought how alluring I looked. If only it was Rob I was pleasing and not Nick. I went downstairs, had another glance at the kitchen mirror, smiled, and then drove my car into Exeter.

I parked outside Nick's apartment and went to his front door. He must have been looking, for he opened the door before I even rang the bell, and there he was, immaculate in a cream linen suit with a softly coloured shirt. He grinned and held out his arms, and before I knew it I was caught in them, his whispering voice in my ears. 'You look stunning, Goldie mine. And that's what I want — to make you really mine.'

I felt quick anger stir inside me but I didn't want to spoil the day, so I wriggled out of his arms, smiled nicely, and walked towards the hotel door. We were met and directed to a discreet table in an alcove, and Nick ordered wine before looking at the menu. He studied it for a long time before looking at me and saying in an almost awed voice, 'Great heavens, this chap is so creative it's almost unbelievable. Look,

Goldie, and choose if you can — it's quite difficult, as you'll see.'

I took the menu and started reading, and understood at once that this was a place quite beyond my liking. Too much expectation, too much pomposity — surely a place where only foodies would come. 'Sea bream salad, please, Nick.'

'But that's boring. Come on, Goldie, choose something more exciting.'

I frowned but kept my voice cool. 'No, that's what I'd like, Nick.'

He sighed, nodded, and raised a hand to summon the waiter. The wine came, and then they discussed the best meal on today's menu. Nick finally decided. 'Reindeer steak with that special sauce. Sounds excellent.'

As time passed, I felt myself relaxing. This wasn't such a bad place after all — welcoming even, although it had a chic and elegant feel to it. I knew I was dressed to suit the ambience, which pleased me. And Nick, talking more quietly now as he enjoyed his reindeer steak, showed me a side of himself far

154

different from the autocratic boss I was used to. He told me how he enjoyed the cookery course he had recently embarked on. 'Who knows — I might turn into a chef after all,' he said with a big grin. 'Run my own little pub somewhere and get a name for my meals.'

I laughed and told him that he would have to get rid of his bouts of temper if he wanted a happy workplace.

'I do try, you know,' he said, refilling my wine glass. 'How's that revolting-looking salad you're halfway through, Goldie?'

I raised my glass to him. 'I'm enjoying it, Nick. And here's to your future — wherever it takes you.'

After coffee in the comfortable lounge and then a wander around the gardens, we drove back to Exeter. I got out of his car and walked towards mine, parked nearby. Then I turned, smiled at him, and said warmly, 'It's been a lovely lunch, Nick. Thanks so much.' Then I added, not really thinking about what I was saying, 'You saved the day for me.'

He smiled back, took a step nearer and looked directly into my eyes. 'Just let me save all your future days, Goldie mine — because you'll be with me from now on. Remember, my love, we're engaged now.'

'What?' My voice reached a pitch I'd never have thought possible. Then I said rapidly, 'Dream on, Nick! You're imagining things. I couldn't possibly marry you!'

13

We were standing there staring at each other. I heard angry surprise in Nick's voice as he said, 'Don't be ridiculous. Of course you will, Goldie.'

'I don't love you, Nick,' I said in a no-nonsense voice. 'I'm sorry, but — '

Suddenly there was an arm around my waist, and a voice I knew cutting in sharply. 'What's all the shouting about? Goldie, are you all right?'

Relief flooded me. I turned quickly, looked into Rob's anxious eyes, and whispered, 'I am now — now that you're here. Please, let's get away.' I saw the expression on his face tighten and feared that a real row might erupt at any moment. One thought came, and words flew into my mouth. 'Gus, let's go to Gus. Oh, Rob, I have to talk to you.'

He didn't ask any more questions. 'Right,' he said firmly, 'I'll drive us there. My car's just here. We'll come and collect yours later. Get in, Goldie, and we'll be off.'

It was such a relief to be away from Nick and his preposterous suggestion. Slowly, beside Rob, I calmed down. Calm enough to turn to him as we drove through the city towards Castle Court and say, 'I thought you were still in London. What happened to bring you back here?'

We went up the hill towards The Studio, and for a moment he didn't reply. Then, parking the car, he turned and looked at me. 'A job down here, starting next week. And then a message from Donna, asking for help as the exhibition gets closer. I can help a bit in what spare time I have.'

My heart sank. He hadn't come back especially to see me on his birthday. It was just because Donna had asked for help. 'Where's the job?' I asked.

He put a hand on mine, clasped in my lap, and his voice warmed. 'Wonderful — Cornwall, if you can believe. Wild birds, misty hills and the ever-present sea. I'm guaranteed to find something worth photographing there, don't you think, Goldie?'

I nodded, unsure how I felt. Pleasure at him being here again; but then I thought about how he'd come to Donna's aid so quickly. But I managed to smile and allow him to press my hand.

He said almost in a whisper, 'Do you want to tell me why you were shouting back there? Why you looked so angry? Until you saw me . . . ' His warm smile lightened the atmosphere building between us. 'Let's go and ask Gus for a cup of something, and then you can tell me everything. Right, Goldie?'

I took up my bag, nodded at him, and felt relieved as we both opened the car doors and got out. Yes, I thought, I would tell him about Nick. But how would he respond to that? I didn't want any more unpleasantness, and certainly not between the two of them.

Rob knocked on The Studio door,

and then we were bathed in the warmth of Gus's welcome. 'Well, the lovebirds! Good to see you — together. Come on in.'

We sat around the cluttered kitchen table, drinking coffee and eating cake. 'Bought it, didn't make it,' Gus told us, grinning. 'So what's the news? Fed up with London, are you, Rob? Can't wait to get back here? Well, it's good to see you. And you, Goldie, my dear.' He looked across the table and smiled. 'Looking prettier than ever. What's the secret, I wonder?'

His faded eyes took on a brighter gleam, and I thought there was only one way I could return all this warmth and care. 'Love,' I said, a bit unsteadily. 'Love, Gus — and it fills me with joy. And of course,' I said lightly, 'new clothes always help.'

'Huh!' He looked embarrassed, and Rob caught my hand under the table. 'Don't make him get emotional — it's not a pretty sight.' And then we were all laughing, and I knew instinctively I had

160

said the right thing to bring us together even more closely.

We talked about Rob's work in London. 'I'm well in with the editor of the magazine,' he said with an enthusiastic smile. 'This, going to Cornwall, is a spin-off, and it looks as if he might keep me on the staff, taking photographs anywhere.' He looked at me and the smile died. 'But of course I'll always keep coming back here.'

To see me? I wondered. Somehow I knew that if I asked why, he would probably remark lightheartedly that he had to visit Rougement Gardens in all seasons; but also because — and I guessed that here his voice would fade until it was only for my ears — 'Always to see you, Goldie.' Of course I didn't ask, and then Gus took our attention, waving a letter under Rob's nose.

'Well, at last something's happening about the house,' he said abruptly. 'I'm to see this chap, the solicitor, tomorrow morning, ten thirty. He phoned and said he had something to tell me. A step in the right direction, he said. Whatever that might mean.' He frowned. 'I don't know why he couldn't have told me over the phone.'

Rob said, 'Because there has to be security about everything the law deals with, Gus. But it sounds hopeful.' They nodded at each other.

'I just hope this step he talks about brings us more information,' Gus said. 'Perhaps news of your missing dad, Rob.'

They exchanged glances. 'It's been a long time, but it's still always at the back of my mind.'

'And mine, lad.'

I heard Gus sigh, I looked at Rob and saw he had a faraway expression on his face, and I decided it was time to stop being nostalgic and take some action. I pushed back my chair, got up and smiled determinedly at both of them. 'Why don't we go out for a cream tea? It's almost tea time.' I glanced at my watch. 'You'll probably feel happier once you've got all those goodies in front of you. Come on, it's my treat.'

In the café, we all cheered up — until Rob said quietly, breaking a pleasant silence while we ate scones, cream and jam, 'What was all that trouble in the car park, Goldie? Who was that chap you were with?'

I poured us second cups of tea and thought hard. Should I tell them about Nick's unseemly proposal? Or should it be kept inside me, a secret to think about and perhaps regret?

Regret? I finished my scone and looked determinedly at Rob, watching me. No, I had no regrets. And it was best that he should know that another man wanted me — more than he did?

So I said in a steady voice, looking into Rob's eyes and hoping I was doing the right thing, 'Nick Burns is my boss, and I've always known he fancied me. And as it was your birthday, Rob, and you had broken our date, and I was disappointed. So I called him and invited him to come out for a meal.'

There was a silence, with both men

staring at me. On Gus's face I saw consternation, and Rob's was expressionless. But only for a moment. Then he frowned, looked at me with amazement, and said, 'What about when you were shouting at him in the car as you were leaving?'

I swallowed the lump forming in my throat and answered tightly, 'It means that he had just told me we were engaged, that I was to marry him, and so I shouted no.'

Another silence. Then Rob reached out take my hand, tightly clasped in my lap. His expression had lightened and so had his voice. 'Thank goodness for that, Goldie. Doesn't sound the sort of man you should marry.' He paused and then added, looking keenly into my eyes, 'Or perhaps he is, and you're not the woman I thought I was getting to know so well.'

This was the moment when I knew that I loved him. It must have shown in my eyes, because suddenly Gus got up and said quickly, 'Sorry, I must go.

Thanks for the tea, Goldie — and I hope you can sort out all these troubles.' He stopped and grinned. 'Don't let things get you down. Rob is here, so what else can you want, eh?' Laughing, he gave us a last wave and left the café.

I was left alone with Rob. We looked at each other, and then slowly we smiled at each other. His hand was warm and strong about mine, and I felt reassurance spread through me. Perhaps now things would work out for the best. Suddenly I remembered the piece of glass in my bag. I got it out, put it on the table between us, and said, 'I found it on the beach. When the sun shines, it looks wonderful. I kept it. It's a charm.'

Rob removed his hand from mine, reached out and stroked the glass. Then he looked at me again. 'It's beautiful, Goldie. Does it work?'

Wanting it near me, I put it into my pocket before answering, and suddenly the words came easily. 'Of course it does. You're here again, and we're together. It's a sort of magic. And that's how charms work.'

He nodded, we smiled at each other, and then I said, 'Time to go. I've got lots of work waiting for me tomorrow.'

'What will the big boss have to say, d'you think?'

I managed a laugh. 'Well, he certainly won't give me the sack. I'm far too valuable to him for that! No, he'll probably ignore everything and we'll go on from there.'

For a moment he was silent. Then he said slowly, with a deeper tone in his voice, 'Have you ever thought of living a different sort of life, Goldie? One where you had no boss, just pleasing yourself and being happy?'

My thoughts whirled. Not another proposal, surely? I laughed, because it was the only thing to do to stop myself wanting, wanting him, so much. 'Look,' I said at last, picking up my bag and pushing back my chair, 'we can't all live your sort of life, Rob. Up and away with the landscape and the birds. I have a good job, and a pleasant flat where I can live and find my happiness in all sorts of things — friends, family, and lots of interests.'

He followed me to the door after I had paid the bill, and we stood outside in the street, looking at the sun touching the cathedral behind us and the people crowding around the green space surrounding it. Then he turned to me, gave me that special smile, and said low, 'Well, just let me know if you change your mind, won't you? I'll give you my new address when I get one. I'm hoping that Gus's talk with the solicitor tomorrow will help move us on towards a finish to the business.'

There was a terrible feeling inside me. He would be going and I would be left behind. But somehow I managed to say, 'Yes, I hope so, too. And if you move, Rob, where will you go? Anywhere in particular?'

He shook his head, still looking into my eyes. 'The world is a large place, and with a camera in my hand I can go anywhere. No plans as yet.' Silence. I felt myself think what was happening and what I could do to make things better. But then, unexpectedly, he put his arms around me, drew me close, and lifted my face towards his. 'But wherever I go, Goldie, I'll always miss you. Remember that, won't you?'

My tight throat was choking. I whispered, 'Yes, Rob, I'll remember that.' And then the words stopped, for his lips were finding mine, and there in the middle of the busy city, we were caught in a close, warm embrace. I had never known anything as wonderful as this before. My heart raced with joy. Could it be that he loved me more than I thought? Should I tell him how I felt and risk the smile on his face fading as he sought for excuses?

But courage failed me. If he was just playing an enjoyable game, then I would seem a fool and he would be embarrassed. Aunt Mary's wise words rang in my head. *If he doesn't love you, let him go.* So I slid out of his arms and said just a bit unsteadily, 'That was lovely. We must do it again sometime. But really, Rob, I have to go home now. Could you please give me a lift back to the car park where I left my car?'

He looked at me with a curious expression on his face, and I wondered if I had spoilt something that might have been really wonderful. But then he nodded and said, 'Of course I will. It's been great seeing you again, and thanks for the tea.' He paused. 'I expect I'll see you around, Goldie. I want to visit your aunt before the exhibition; perhaps we might meet there, one evening next week?'

'Good idea,' I said brightly. 'Shall we make it Tuesday, around sixish?'

'Sure. I'll be there. He smiled and then we walked together back to the car park, and I knew I had thrown away my dream of loving him.

14

There was a letter waiting for me when I reached home. *Looks formal*, I thought. *Who on earth is writing to me?*

It was an invitation from Donna to visit the opening of the gallery, just like the one Aunt Mary had received. Quickly I wrote an equally formal response and marked the date in my diary.

In the morning, Nick called me into his office brandishing the same invitation I had received last night. 'What's all this, Goldie?' he asked. 'How did these people get my name? How do they know anything about me?' He glared across his desk. 'Something to do with you, is it?'

I sat down opposite him and smiled. 'Don't go on so, Nick. Yes, it's an exhibition of a portrait belonging to my aunt. I expect the curator discovered that I knew you, and so here you are with an invitation.' I looked at him a little more warmly. 'Why not accept and allow yourself to do something new?'

He waited, and I saw uncertainly fill his face. And then he smiled, that amused smile that meant he thought I was a fool but he was too polite to say so. 'All right,' he said. 'And you can come with me — how's that? I don't know a thing about art, so you can explain it as we go.'

It was my turn to frown. 'Sorry, but I'm taking my aunt in a wheelchair. I'll have to be with her.'

His smile was pleasant and his voice sounded friendlier. 'Then I'll come with you — old ladies and I usually get on well. So that's settled — and now can we get back to work? Have a nice trip down to Cornwall next week; just don't spend all day there, will you?'

I had to smile. Cornwall! And then I thought, *Rob said he was going to Cornwall — if only we could go together.* But no, that was a dream.

I hurried out of Nick's office and immersed myself in work. Yes, the next visit was to a small cottage near St Methyr. For a moment I sat back and shut my eyes. Cliff House was still happily occupied by yet another lot of holidaymakers, and apart from Flo's cottage, I hadn't seen another building close to it. But it would be exciting to find it. I told myself to stop dreaming and get on with the work. But I paused for another moment and fingered the piece of green glass, always in my pocket now. The charm. I smiled to myself, shook my head, and dived into yet another file.

Tuesday came, and I looked forward to seeing Rob when we visited Aunt Mary. And yet a part of me was embarrassed by what had happened only yesterday. Would he have forgotten that kiss? Had it been just a modern friendly gesture? It couldn't have meant anything deeper, could it?

We met at the suggested time, and I thought he looked just a bit happier than usual. On the drive to Riverside, I dared to ask him what news Gus had learned about his missing father. He smiled and nodded his head. 'A step further along that tricky path,' he said. He glanced towards me as I turned down the drive to Riverside. 'I'll tell you later. Perhaps we could have a drink in the local pub before going home?'

Aunt Mary looked pale, but that was her usual colour. And, as she welcomed us and began talking about the exhibition, a flush came into her cheeks and a rising note in her quiet voice. 'That nice young woman, the one who's the curator at the gallery, came a few days ago and asked me if there were any photographs I could share with them. And then I recalled the old album in the drawer over there . . . ' A frail hand pointed to the chest of drawers on the far side of the room, and she looked at me, nodded, and said excitedly, 'Goldie, see if it's there, please.'

I went across, opened the drawer and, yes, amongst a neat pile of old letters and some crumpled papers lay a photograph album. I took it to her and sat down again. I looked at Rob and he raised an eyebrow and smiled back, and I knew he was as excited as I was.

We watched Aunt Mary adjust her spectacles, open the book and then turn the pages. For a few moments there was silence in the room, until she found what she was looking for. 'There he is! Charles Mason, who painted the portrait. Her voice faded. 'I'll never forget him.'

I took the album from her and looked carefully at the photo of a handsome man in his army uniform. Thickset, with a determined expression on his good-looking face. Automatically, I thought, *Indeed, he's someone you'd never forget. Poor Aunt Mary.* Then I became interested in the background of the photo. Charles Mason stood outside the open door of a small cottage, with a view behind him of a long beach with sunshine making the white curling waves look even more brilliant. I lifted my head, met Rob's eyes, and then looked at her. 'This was his home, Aunt?' I asked softly, not wanting to interrupt the memories.

'Yes,' she said, her voice low. 'His studio, close to the beach. He worked there, you see.'

I nodded. 'You think Donna would like to see this?'

The thought was irritating, but it pleased me to see her face lift, eyes glinting as if she were a young girl again, as she nodded and said softly, 'I would love the world to see this man, this great artist, so when they look at the portrait of the three girls, they'll understand more easily what it was like to live at that time.'

Rob was smiling in that gentle way I so loved as he looked at Aunt Mary and said, 'Thank you, Mrs Seaton, for your generosity and understanding. I know Donna will be delighted to have a photo of the artist to help bring the portrait of the girls to life. May I take it and give it to her when I go to the gallery tomorrow?'

A nod, a smile, and the photo was handed to him. 'Take care of it,' she murmured.

Rob said quickly, 'It's so precious that I'll put it in my uncle's safe as soon as I get back tonight.'

Aunt Mary lay back in her chair. She looked tired and overexcited, I thought. It was time for us to go. With the photo safely placed in a large strong envelope, we got ready to leave her room.

'See you again soon,' I said softly. 'And then we must make arrangements for you to come to the gallery. Goodnight, dear Aunt.'

She merely waved, and I saw her eyelids drop into sleep as we left the room. Outside in the car park, Rob said, 'I know a good pub where we can talk. Okay with you, Goldie?'

'That sounds nice. Hold on to that photo, won't you?'

He nodded, and I watched as he

slipped the envelope into the car pocket and then lock the door. 'Drive me there, will you, Goldie? And then we'll come back here and I'll pick up mine. The pub's not far away. Ready?'

I slid into the passenger seat and we were away. The Old Oak pub stood beside the river. A few boats sculled about, and people sat on benches chatting and laughing as the sun slowly sank beyond the horizon. A good place, I thought, for whatever Rob had to tell me.

I nursed my glass of apple juice in both hands and looked at him. 'So tell me the news, Rob. I do hope it's good. I want to know how Gus got on with the solicitor.'

Rob put down his tankard and stretched his legs out on the grass beneath our bench. He nodded, moved an inch or two closer to me, and looked intently into my eyes. He said, 'It's sort of half-and-half good news, really. You see, they've got information about my father.'

15

I felt excitement throb through my body. But my doubtful thoughts said warily, *What can the bad news be?* I said nothing, just looked at Rob; and then, almost without knowing, reached for his hand and held it in mine. Seeing his expression warming, I whispered, 'Tell me, Rob. Tell me.'

He looked down at our clasped hands and then into my eyes, and said gently, 'You have a magical piece of glass, Goldie, but you're *my* charm. Always loving, always ready to listen. I think of you as my best friend.'

I swallowed and then carefully slipped my hand out of his. I sat back on the bench, and my thoughts, although saddened by these words, came to my aid. After all, a best friend was someone who would always be there; who always, as he said, would listen. And help if possible. It didn't really rely on love, did it?

For a long moment he just sat there, seemingly lost in thought. But then he turned to look into my eyes as he said, his voice low but tinged with something I hadn't heard before, 'My father has been found, but he died last month. In Australia. So no wonder we couldn't trace him.'

What could I say? Just, 'I'm so sorry, Rob. And Gus will be upset, I'm sure.'

'Yes.'

I thought of Gus, who must be glad to have news of his brother, even if it was so sad; and suddenly I wanted to be there in his studio, talking to him, perhaps cheering him up if I could. The idea was so alive that I said quickly, 'Rob, let's go back to the studio, shall we? I'm sure Gus would be glad to see us. What do you think?'

He didn't answer at once, and I saw thoughts sweeping across his face. But then he smiled, got up from the bench, and looked down at me. 'That's a good idea, Goldie. But I feel I must get to the gallery. I know Donna will be working this evening, and I'd like to give her this photo of Mason. Do you mind? And you could see Gus another day? Or even now, without me?'

The finality of his words hit me painfully. But I stood up, shouldered my bag and somehow managed to give him a bright, understanding smile. 'Yes, that's what I might do, Rob. And of course it would be best to hand over the precious photo as soon as you can.'

He looked relieved. 'That's great. And tomorrow I'll be off to Cornwall. I heard today that a rare bird's been seen there, so I must get a pic if I can.' His smile grew. 'Might even be my competition winner! Wish me luck, Goldie?'

I nodded and forced myself to speak normally. 'That sounds terrific. And I'm sure Gus would be thrilled if you did win. I'll keep my charm shining for you.'

Back in the car park, he hesitated before getting into his car. He looked at me, pausing before he said fondly, 'How lucky I am to have you, Goldie. You always understand, and that's what I need. My best friend.' He kissed me on both cheeks, smiling, his hands palming mine and pressing them.

I couldn't take any more. Smiling back, feeling my face stiff and taut, I went back to my own car and quickly drove away.

The next morning — a sunny day, with its shafts of golden light drifting through my windows — I felt the world was too bright for me. My thoughts were grey. Why couldn't everything match them? While I mixed fruit and cereal for my breakfast, I put the glass charm on the table and looked at it. I sighed. Did I really think it was a charm? It hadn't produced any magic so far. And then, as I drained my coffee, its new brightness caught my eye. Sunshine gleamed on it, and no longer just a bit of smooth glass from the beach, it showed itself true and lovely. Full of hope. Something to wish upon.

It helped me to recover from my grim view of the world. I was smiling as I put it back in my pocket and faced the new day waiting for me.

I managed to call on Gus in my lunch hour. He welcomed me and I went in, not quite sure what to say. But he seemed brighter than usual, grinning and saying, 'Coffee? I must tell you the latest news. Or has Rob told you?'

I tightened my fingers, holding the charm in my pocket, and said as lightly as I could manage, 'Yes, he has. About your brother. Of course, I'm so sorry that you found out he passed away. I know you made a long search to find him, so this must be painful.' I paused, and then added, 'If there's anything I can do to help, Gus, you only have to say so.'

He poured the coffee and found a tin of biscuits, pushing it over the table towards me. I thought his eyes looked watery, but his grin remained as he said, 'I don't know what we'd do without you now, Rob and me.'

I caught my breath and could only murmur unsteadily, 'But it's such a pleasure to know you.' I paused. 'And Rob, of course.'

He was watching me, and I realised that my thoughts were an open book to such a wise old man. After stirring sugar into his coffee, he looked across at me again. 'The boy's slowly coming to his senses, thank goodness. Once all the money business is cleared up, I just hope he'll settle down.'

The expression on his face told me just what those careful words concealed. But I had no reply to give him, even though I rubbed the glass charm with even stronger fingers, asking it to help me bring this painful conversation to an end. I said more brightly, 'Yes, of course — the money. Do you know now what's to happen about it?' Then felt embarrassed at such a probing question. This inheritance was nothing to do with me, and it was only through Gus's good nature that I had learned about the death of his brother. I muttered something about being sorry and that it was none of my business.

He smiled at me. 'Of course it's your business, Goldie. If Rob and I inherit the money that goes with Cliff House, I'll let him have it all, and then I'm pretty sure he'll want to settle somewhere.' He nodded, and then added with that amused look in his eyes, 'Cornwall, I wouldn't be surprised. Even Cliff House itself. And because you're his best friend — yes, he told me that — he'll need you to be near to him, to listen to all his new complaints and worries.'

I couldn't help it — I laughed. Really, Gus was going beyond the permitted boundaries! I watched his face, and how he laughed with me, but then the smile faded and his voice dropped. 'Love is a strange thing. Sometimes it works, other times it doesn't. But you're a sensible woman, and I feel sure you'll sort out everything in time. Now . . . ' He got up and I followed him. He put his arm around my shoulders as we walked down the hall towards the door. Opening it, he gave me one of his enigmatic looks, but there was warmth on his face and in his voice. 'If that lad can ever admit he loves you, then be sure that my love goes along with his. Now off you go, and stop worrying.'

I drove down to Cornwall to keep my afternoon appointment. Flo was there to welcome me, of course; and as we drank tea in her kitchen, she told me about the cottage I had come to inspect. 'The Old Coastguard Cottage, that's what it's called. Funny old place, almost on the beach. Hasn't been lived in for years. Not since the war, when he died, poor man.' She stirred her tea.

I caught my thoughts together. He must be Charles Mason — Aunt Mary had told me he lived down here, and painted in what he called his studio. Yes, of course, Coastguard Cottage. I took papers and photographs out of my bag and looked at the small building, with the shining sea surrounding it, and felt a sudden warm emotion sweep through me. Here was where Aunt Mary's tales came to life. Quickly I finished my tea, got Flo to sign her part of the contract — for she had agreed to be caretaker until new occupants arrived — and then said, 'Sorry, Flo, can't stop. Must go and look around before the tide turns and sweeps me away!'

We laughed, and I hugged her farewell. What a blessing to have Flo here, in this beautiful place so full of memories.

Walking along the clifftop, I found a small rough path leading down into the beach, which took me to the door of the cottage. The key grated in the lock, and the place smelled musty; I remembered Flo saying it had remained empty since Charles Mason's death, and that was a long time ago. Looking about me, I knew it would need a lot of renovation before it could welcome holidaymakers. But the place had a special feel to it, and a sudden thought came into my mind as I left, locking the door behind me. Aunt Mary and Charles had been together here. I smiled to myself as I guessed that the old cottage had been their haven of love.

Back in Torquay, I took out my invitation to the exhibition on Wednesday evening and tried to think sensibly about taking Aunt Mary there. A phone call to Matron at Riverside, and a message to Aunt Mary, and it was all arranged. I would pick her up, with her wheelchair in the back of the car, and take her to Exeter. There, with any luck, I could park outside the gallery for a few minutes while I wheeled her into the lobby and hope someone would welcome her until I could come back from finding a legal parking space. It all seemed quite clear, and I knew I was looking forward to taking her there.

And then, relaxing in the kitchen after supper, I thought more deeply. Seeing the portrait of the three girls again would surely bring memories back to her mind. And if, as Donna planned, there would also be explanations about the actual girls as they grew up and faced life in the war, I hoped that all this return to the past wouldn't be too much for her. But she was eager to go, so I knew we must just see what happened.

Then my thoughts swung to the possibility of seeing Rob, and Donna. He had said he was off to Cornwall a few days ago, but of course he must have returned and was, I imagined, even now helping Donna put everything into place. I sat on, nursing my cooling cup of coffee and staring out of the window. All I saw was rooftops; all I heard was the noise of cars on the busy road below. I felt alone and sad that things were turning out in a different way from how I'd hoped.

Putting my hand into my pocket, I took out the glass charm and sat it on the table in front of me. It shone, I thought, as the fading sunlight drifted through the window. But I didn't see that rich gleam of green light when the sun shone on it. Getting up, because it was no good just sitting and feeling miserable, I went into my bedroom and tried to decide what to wear to the exhibition. Not that it could possibly matter, I thought. Rob would have no eyes for me, not as he accompanied Donna around the various rooms.

But then I cheered up a bit. At least he would be there. He would talk to me. I smiled to myself. His best friend, he had told me. I would hear his voice, and see his lovely sea-green eyes light up as we greeted each other, and that would have to be enough.

16

Aunt Mary was ready for me. She sat up straight in her chair and her eyes gleamed. She said brightly, 'Here I am, dear child. All ready for my visit to the exhibition. If you help me, I can manage to go down to your car. But I can't walk along streets, so I'm afraid it's the wheelchair to get me there.'

I kissed her. 'It's no problem, dear Aunt Mary. We can manage well. And my goodness, don't you look smart!'

She chuckled. 'I had my hair done, and asked for it to look a bit more modern — and this is the result. I'm quite pleased with it.'

'I think it looks attractive. And that dress is really lovely. Have I seen it before?'

Another chuckle. 'It's years old, my dear — just hanging there unworn. So I thought I'd give it an outing today.'

I nodded. The soft silk print with its gentle blue and green colours suited her, and I wondered if this was how she must have looked when she and Charles Mason were together. I said, 'It's beautiful, Aunt Mary, and I know you'll be the belle of the ball at the gallery.'

We shared a good laugh then, but it was time to move. With the help of her stick in one hand and the other tucked into my arm, we went slowly out of her room and took the stair lift downstairs. Matron stood by the door, beaming. 'Have a good time, Mrs Seaton, and you can tell us all about it when you get back.'

'I will — oh, I will!'

I could tell that she enjoyed our drive into the city, for she rarely had outings. Finally I parked as near to the gallery as possible, saying, 'Sit tight, Aunt Mary. I'll get the wheelchair out of the boot.' When it was ready, I brought it to the side door and helped her into it.

'Goodness,' she said, looking around

her, 'what a change. It was never as big as this when I was last here.'

I wheeled her into the building, wondering how long ago that was and whether Charles Mason had been with her. But this was no time for such thoughts, for a pleasant young man at the door was taking our invitations and smiling as he directed us into the main hall. 'Miss Adams will be in there in a minute, and I know she'll be glad to welcome you, Mrs Seaton.'

I wheeled Aunt Mary into the large airy hallway. The walls were bare, but plaster casts of famous men and women were arranged on the many pieces of antique furniture. Groups of talking people were strolling about, looking at these casts, and the vast room echoed with their voices. I saw Aunt Mary looking around her with an expression of wonder, but then suddenly there was a familiar voice in our ears.

'Mrs Seaton, and oh yes, of course, your niece. Er — Ms Smith, isn't it?'

I nodded, and thought that Donna's

brief smile meant nothing. She came closer, put a hand on the handle of the wheelchair and said, 'It will be my great pleasure to show you around, Mrs Seaton.' Then she turned to me and said, 'We'll be back in time for tea. I'm sure you can amuse yourself until then — Goldie, isn't it?'

By now I was angry indeed, but knew I mustn't explode and spoil Aunt Mary's visit. So I said coldly, 'Thank you so much — er, Donna, isn't it? I'll go and look at the craft exhibits.' I leant down and whispered in Aunt Mary's ear, 'Have a good time,' and watched as Donna, smiling more pleasantly now, wheeled her out of the hall and into what I supposed was where the exhibition was set up.

I went slowly to look at the craft room, and then suddenly someone behind me said, 'Looks as if you're lost, Goldie. Never mind, I'll keep you company.'

I swung round, hoping to see Rob; but it was Nick, grinning at me and taking my arm as he marched me out of the hall and into a large room lined with local crafts. I turned to him and asked sharply, 'Why are you here? You don't know anything about art.'

He raised an eyebrow and let his smile shine out. 'What a welcome! Thanks a lot. But you told me so much about this famous artist that I'm ready to learn.'

I looked at him and realised my sharpness was uncalled for. Nick was a nice man, once you got used to his outbursts of quick temper. I said more quietly, 'Why don't we go and look at his portrait? It's in that big room, along with other local works.'

'And your aunt? I'm looking forward to meeting her.'

I wasn't sure if he meant this, but by now we had reached the exhibition and I felt speech fade away. The walls were lined with amazing pictures, and as I moved around and read the names, I realised I knew a couple of them. Men and women who I had grown up with, often painting at school, and here they were showing what they had achieved. This gave me a new thought — if you stuck to what you could do, who knew what the product might be? Like Rob and his photography. For a moment I felt old doubts surface, but then, moving around the room, I found myself beside Donna, who stood close to Aunt Mary and was bending down and talking to her.

'Yes, Mrs Seaton,' she said, 'I presumed to collect a few more details about your friends, the Crosby girls, including these old photographs. Here you can see them as they grew up and worked through the war. So interesting, and I do hope the visiting viewers will appreciate how women lived in the past.'

Aunt Mary mumbled something I couldn't hear, but I knew what I was going to say. Inside me, resentment grew, and the words tumbled out fast. 'Where did you get these photos? Have you been bothering poor Aunt Mary again, when I wasn't about?' My anger grew. 'And if so, how dare you!'

Donna looked at me and frowned; but then the chilly smile came out again. 'What a storm in a teacup, Goldie. No, I researched the girls on my computer and found all about their wartime experiences online, and photos of them wearing clothes of the period. Have a look and forget how cross you are!'

So I looked, and did indeed nearly forget my anger with her. The big portrait of the girls almost filled a panel in the white wall; and around it, neatly framed and clearly presented, were the photos she had found. Harriet, a nurse, looking serious and efficient. Rose in her skimpy bright dress, pouting and smiling into the camera. And then, in dull clothes, Edwina, a farmer's wife with a basket of something in her hands. When the shock of seeing this had left me, I leaned over the back of the chair.

'What do you think, Aunt Mary? Is

this how they looked? I hope you're not shocked to see them here.'

It took a few moments for her to reply, and when she did her voice was faint. 'I can't imagine how you found them, Miss Adams — but, yes, it's wonderful to see them. And to read how they lived and worked in those terrible times.'

I nodded and then heard Nick say, 'You're quite right, of course, Aunt Mary.' *How dare he call her that*, I thought, but he was going on. 'I'm Nick Burns, Goldie's boss, and I'm delighted to meet you. Now, may I have the pleasure of taking you in to tea?'

I know my mouth dropped open, and then I shook my shoulders and allowed a small smile to spread across my face. 'Nick,' I said, 'it's kind of you to offer, but I think I'll take Aunt Mary. I'm used to the wheelchair, and I don't want you driving her as you usually drive.'

Thank goodness there was a small chuckle from everyone gathered around, and Aunt Mary smiled and nodded her head. 'It was very good of you to offer, Mr Burns. But as Goldie says, she and I will go together.'

As I took hold of the chair, she looked back at the portrait and said so quietly I hardly heard her, 'Perhaps we could come back after tea — for a last look.'

The tea room was pleasantly laid out, with individual tables and chairs set about the long table in the centre. Aunt Mary was greeted by a matronly woman who was pouring tea, and we found our way to a small table in a niche by the long window that over-looked Rougement Gardens. I thought it was an ideal place, and an ideal time. Aunt Mary needed to rest after all the excitement, and I had been so surprised by Nick's charming behaviour that I felt I would like to sit down and think. And my thoughts, as ever, turned to Rob. Where was he? I had imagined he would be at Donna's side, talking to visitors and explaining some of the pictures. But there was no sign of him at all.

I turned my thoughts back to Aunt Mary, who sipped her tea with a faraway look in her eyes. I said gently, 'I hope it wasn't all too much for you, dear Aunt? All those photos, and the descriptions going with them. I had no idea Donna would do this. I hope they haven't upset you.'

Slowly she shook her head and put the cup down on the table. 'No, my dear. Despite the surprise, I'm delighted that Miss Adams went to all that trouble. It really brought new life back to my old memories. But . . . ' She smiled, looking a bit fragile, I thought, and then said, 'I'm ready to go back to Riverside. Please could you take me now? But first, of course, I must thank Miss Adams.'

'Yes,' I said, wondering who would look after her as I went to bring the car as close as possible to the door. 'I'll take you back to the portrait room, and Donna will be there. And then . . . ' A voice interrupted me and I saw Nick come to Aunt Mary's side.

'Anything I can do to help, Mrs Seaton?'

I thought quickly and smiled up at him. 'Take my keys and go and move my car to the door, Nick — that would be really good.'

He grinned. 'As good as done. Let's have them, then.' He gave one of his more charming smiles to Aunt Mary and said briefly, 'I'll be back in a moment. Just stay put.'

She and I looked at each other and then laughed. 'What a nice man,' she said, raising her eyebrows at me so that I knew exactly what she was thinking. A possible husband, no doubt.

I hurried her back to take a last look at the portrait and the photos, and then Nick was at the door, handing over my keys and asking, 'What next, madam? Any other little jobs I can help you with?'

I smiled my thanks. 'Nick, you're a star. And yes, go and fetch Aunt Mary while I open the car door, will you?'

With a bit of fuss and manoeuvring, she got into in the passenger seat with the wheelchair in the boot, and I moved in beside her. Lowering the window, I looked at Nick and said with amusement, 'What will you be doing next?'

His grin was mocking as he smiled and said, 'Going to chat up the lovely Donna, of course. What else did you expect? I'll tell you about it tomorrow.'

It had been a wonderful afternoon, and I knew Aunt Mary had enjoyed it. Back in her room, she sat in her comfortable chair and smiled at me. 'Thank you,' she said simply. 'You're such a good girl, Goldie. And what nice people were there — your Mr Burns, and Miss Adams. But I expected to see Mr Tyson, too. Do you know where he might be?'

'I believe he has some business to attend to with his uncle, but I expect he'll soon be around again. Now good night, Aunt Mary, and sleep well. I'll be back in a day or two.'

As I left her, I saw her eyes close, and knew that she would be reliving those days when she and Charles Mason were together. Driving back to Torquay, I couldn't help wishing that Rob and I could make a few happy memories. But I remembered Aunt Mary's wise words then — *If he doesn't love you, then let him go.*

Impossible, I thought wearily. But perhaps it was the best thing to do.

17

The next morning I took the glass charm out of my pocket and looked at it keenly. Finishing my breakfast, I put it back again, muttering, 'Time for you to do some good, please,' and then thought how stupid I was to really believe a bit of glass could help in any way.

In the office, I found Nick grinning at me as he came into my room and, with a sinking heart, guessed I was going to hear about his exploits of the evening before. But instead he stood behind my chair with a hand on my shoulder and said, 'Goldie, you work so hard, and you're so good at your job. And on top of that, all the help you give your aunt . . . Well, I think you deserve a reward. How about taking a holiday?'

I turned to stare at him. 'A holiday?' I muttered. 'Well, of course, but how? I mean, what? And who'd do my work while I was away?'

He grinned again. 'Ways and means. I have a niece who needs a job — she can learn here as she goes along. Just leave her some helpful notes and I think she'll be fine.'

I took a long breath. A holiday. Of course that would be great. As I expelled the breath, my excitement grew. I would go to Cornwall. To stay with Flo Bailey if she would have me. And then I would be able to look at Cliff House and do some more dreaming. And perhaps Rob would find me there . . .

'Right,' I said briskly, collecting papers and switching off the computer. 'I'd like to go right now — okay with you, Nick? And I'll write notes for your . . . ' I smiled sweetly. 'Your niece, was it?'

His grin died and he looked slightly bemused. 'Of course she's my niece. I can't think what you're suggesting, Goldie,' he blustered.

Getting up from my desk, I said, 'I know you have lots of nieces, so I'm wondering which one it will be.' And after a moment's pause, we smiled at each other.

'You're too bright, my girl. All right, it's someone I met last night. At the party Donna gave.' He walked with me to the door. 'Not as pretty as you. Perhaps a bit easier to get on with. Fingers crossed it'll work out all right. Wish me luck, Goldie.'

I couldn't help it; I kissed him on the cheek. He deserved to find someone who would put up with him. 'Okay, Nick. I'm off. Back in two weeks' time, yes?'

He nodded, then slowly walked towards his office. I heard the door shut with a bang, and as I walked down the stairs, I wished the 'niece' good luck with her new job.

At home I rang Flo's number and, hearing her voice, felt a great warmth inside me. She was delighted, she said, to offer me bed and breakfast for as long as I cared to stay. 'My last lot of holidaymakers left at the weekend. It'll be lovely to see you, Goldie.'

'Thanks, Flo. I'll be with you tomorrow afternoon.'

At once I started packing. Not many clothes, and nearly all of them beach gear. *Don't forget the swimming costume.* This afternoon I would go and see Aunt Mary, tell her I would be away for a few days, and make sure she had everything she wanted. And then it hit me — her birthday was in ten days' time. Her hundredth birthday! Of course I would be back in time for that.

She seemed in good spirits when I arrived later that afternoon. 'Dear Goldie, thank you for that wonderful visit to the gallery. I did so enjoy it — all the photos, and such nice people all around me. But I do feel tired. I'm dozing off quite a lot.'

I put my arms around her. 'That's allowed, dear Aunt. As long as you're wide awake for that important birthday coming up.'

'Yes, something else to look forward to. How lucky I am.' After leaving my address at Flo's cottage with Matron, I went back to the car, and knew I wanted to go and see Gus. To try and understand just what he and Rob were doing, and where and when.

There was no reply to my knock at the door — three knocks. Then someone appeared from the house next door and said, 'Looking for Gus, are you? Gone off he has, with the lad. Something to do in London, he said. Won't be back for a few days.' Disappointment hit me, but I thanked the chap for his information and went back to the car.

All sorts of thoughts bounded around in my head. London meant more inheritance business. But Rob had a commission to do in Cornwall. Little chance of him being there when I was then, within the next week. So why was I going to Cornwall tomorrow?

I drove home slowly and then sat about in the flat, wondering what my life was up to, making me so confused. But gradually, as I picked at my supper, I knew I had one good thing to do — buy a present for Aunt Mary. And I would buy it in Cornwall. There were lots of galleries and craft shops down there, and I would be sure to find something she would like. That cheered me up, and I went to bed feeling a bit happier.

The morning dawned with a cloudy sky outside my window, and again I wondered if I really needed a holiday. And why go to Cornwall? But the green glass, on the table as I ate my breakfast, shined most attractively, as if to say, *Come on, it's not as bad as you think.*

Of course, it wasn't bad at all. A drive down through Devon's green lanes and across the shining river, and then the feeling that I always had — *Cornwall is so different from Devon. And I love it.*

Flo seemed delighted to welcome me, and we sat down at her long pine table eating mackerel fresh from the sea that morning. 'Young Matt Broom caught these; said he had a lot of them, and would I like a couple? Course I said yes — I knew you'd enjoy it.'

We sat there when we'd finished the meal, and gossiped. I told her a bit about Aunt Mary and the Crosby girls, who once lived in Cliff House, and then she told me all about the last tenants, who had been so happy there. 'Wanted to stay for ever, they did. But I don't suppose they could afford it. So it'll be another lot of people arriving soon.'

I nodded, but didn't say a word about Gus and Rob becoming owners of the old house. They would, I guessed, sell it and then go their separate ways; Rob probably to London, or even on trips around the world with his camera, and Gus staying in Castle Court and painting his daubs.

I smiled at the absurdity of my thoughts — how could I possibly know what might happen next? Flo looked at me with keen eyes. 'Look as if a holiday would do you good, my lover. Life been a bit busy lately, has it?'

'Yes, Flo, it has. And now that I'm here, I don't know what to do next.'

She got up and pushed the old chair away. 'Come upstairs and look at your room, that's what you can do.'

We went up the narrow creaking stairs, and then she opened the door of a small room tucked under the thatched eaves. I heard birds feeding their young and imagined those cosy little nests under centuries of thatch. It was a lovely little room, instantly welcoming and airy.

Flo was watching me. She smiled as she headed back to the kitchen. 'I thought you'd like it. All my guests said it was a nice room. Now have a rest until tea time, when I'll call you down.'

The door creaked shut behind her and I sat on the bed, wondering if I really did need a rest. But then memories sparked, and I knew what I wanted to make me feel good — a walk along the cliffs. Views of the landscape, hard and rugged, with the ocean throwing spray with each huge wave. All that fresh, sweet air would surely blow away my unhappy thoughts.

And it did. After walking from the big beach below the house to the next tiny cove, I sat down on turf pink with thrift flowers, and felt much better. Looking down, I stared at the greeny blue sea with its lacy white scallops of waves, and told myself that tomorrow I would ask Flo for a picnic and sit on the beach before swimming.

I was smiling brightly when I returned to the cottage and shared another meal with Flo. We chatted during the evening, but I was ready for an early night, and so excused myself just as it was getting dark. 'Sleep well, lover,' she said, and I knew I would.

I was awake early and lay there, happy to be at peace with the world. It was lovely not to have to rush to go to work, that busy car journey every morning, and the same queues at going-home time. Here was quiet and contentment.

I heard a knock at the door and there

was Flo, bringing me a cup of tea. I grinned at her. 'I'll come and stay again, Flo. What a wonderful landlady you are!'

She nodded her head. 'So they all say. Now take your time; you've got all day waiting for you.'

As I got up, I thought, *If only Rob was waiting for me, too, that would be perfect*; but of course he was with Gus in London. Perhaps tomorrow he might come and look for me. Unless he had other things to do.

Later, as the sun began to shine through small drifting clouds, I shouldered the bag containing my swimming gear and Flo's picnic, and set out on my adventure. The glass stone was in my pocket, and I told myself to cheer up — this was going to be a good day.

A salty breeze ruffled my hair, shells on the tide line were waiting to be collected, and the music of the sea quietly called me to join it and see what magic there was in swimming among its waves. In one of the rock pools where I idled, searching for shrimps and pretty sea anemones, I found a dead jellyfish, but took little notice of it. Cornwall, I knew, was renowned for all the strange things that washed up on its beaches. And why wasn't I actually in the water?

Swimming costume on, hair tied up and shoes off, I went down into the curling waves, noticing that the water was warmer than I expected, and then plunged in and swam. It took a minute or so to get my breath, to remember just how to swim properly. All the doubts and unhappiness disappeared in the joy of the moment. I felt I could stay out here forever and let the waves wash away all my sadness.

Then something surfaced near me. I turned my head sharply. A dolphin, perhaps? A seal? Even one of those nasty jellyfish with long tentacles and a sting if it got too near you? I heaved in a big breath, decided not to be afraid, and turned to look at what was happening beside me.

I saw a head, with dark hair plastered

down, bright eyes glinting at me, the same colour as the sea. A voice saying, 'Goldie? So here you are!'

It was Rob. He had come and found me. He was here in the water, looking at me with an expression I hadn't seen before.

'Goldie,' he said again. 'I knew I'd find you down here. Something to do with your magic charm, I guess?'

I knew my smile must be telling him just how happy I was to see him, but I had no words. And then I realised we didn't need words. We were together, and there were other ways of telling him how much I loved him. My wet hands encircled his head, pulling him down deep into the water; and there, in the depths of the embracing waves, I kissed him.

18

Breathe, breathe! We were both breath-
less when we finally surfaced, shaking
our heads to get rid of the water, and
smiling into each other's eyes. Then,
suddenly despite my joy, I realised I had
thrown myself at him. What must he
think of me? But this wasn't the time to
talk about it. Instead I turned away
from him, shouted, 'Race you to the
beach,' and set off, hoping he would
follow.

He did, but he let me win the race, so
by the time I was scrabbling up the
beach to where my towel waited, I'd
had time to try and calm down. I
smiled at him as he joined me, finding a
towel in the backpack that lay beside
my basket. He grinned, saying, 'What
talents, Goldie! I didn't realise you were
a channel swimmer as well as all the
other things!'

I sat down on the warm golden sand, towelling my hair, and avoided his eyes as I said, 'It's that magic charm, making me seem like somebody else with far more talent than I have.' I looked up at him. 'Sit down, Rob. How did you find me? Has someone been telling on me?'

'Flo Bailey,' he answered, pulling the towel around his chest. 'I asked her, 'Have you seen a pretty woman with golden hair anywhere around?' And with a twinkle in her eyes she told me, 'Must be Goldie, and she's staying here. But try the beach, lad. Gone swimming, she has.' So I came down and there you were, a mermaid among the waves.'

We shared a laugh. Then he turned towards me.

'I've missed seeing you. But you've been in my mind all the time. And now . . . ' He stopped, put down his towel and moved a little closer to me. ' . . . I've got to go away again. Those damned birds are calling me!' Despite his laugh, I saw how his emotions swept across his face, which gave me a chance to share my own feelings.

'You and your birds,' I said softly, returning his smile. 'Where are you off now? Did you photograph the rare birds you talked about last week? Or perhaps you're off on a safari in the African jungle?'

He leaned towards me, took my hands, and smoothed them with his thumbs, smiling back. 'If I ever go on safari, I'll insist you come with me. And the rare birds are still there, not far away. Somewhere on the cliffs around the Lizard peninsula.'

We looked at each other, and his fingers around my hands grew stronger. Warmer. Meaning something, I knew. My words came out without thought. 'I love you, Rob, and I don't want you to go anywhere without me.'

And then his arms, still damp, were around me, pulling me close, closer. We kissed, and I felt the touch of sand on his lips. When we drew apart, I said breathlessly, 'What a pair of water babies we are!'

We laughed, and I think we both knew something important had grown between us. Feeling relaxed and happy, I opened the basket Flo had given me, and there was our picnic.

Rob edged away far enough to take the sandwich I handed him. But I knew that he was at last able to be frank with me. We had both declared ourselves, and now we could share this moment, wonderful as it was.

Words bubbled up inside me. Happy words, words that meant little but everything at the same time. 'Now you're here,' I said lightly, 'let's spend time with each other. I'll come with you to find the birds you have to photograph — and then . . . '

'And then?' he asked, eyes dancing.

I offered him a bun packed with cheese and chutney. 'Lots of things, Rob. I have to buy a present for Aunt Mary — her birthday next week — and there are so many lovely craft pieces to buy in Cornwall. We can have a good look around. Will you come with me?'

For a moment he was silent. He took a mouthful of the bun, chewed it, and then looked at me in a different way. 'A good look around? Yes, Goldie, that's what we'll do. And there's one special place we must go to — can you guess where?'

I poured out mugs of coffee and handed him one. 'Sounds mysterious, Rob! Don't tease. Tell me, please.'

'Well, it's to do with your Aunt Mary. You see, Flo didn't have a spare room, and she told me that the coastguard cottage is empty, so I parked my sleeping bag there, and I'll be tucked away among the spiders while you sleep in comfort with Flo telling you old stories!'

I looked at him with surprise. The coastguard cottage? But that was where Charles Mason lived and worked — and Aunt Mary visited him there. Suddenly I longed to go and look at it. I jumped to my feet and said quickly, 'I want to see it, Rob. You see, it's got such a history.'

'Yes, I imagine it has. The artist and your young aunt? Come on, then!'

We left the picnic basket safely tucked away behind rocks, and I watched Rob take his camera from his backpack. He nodded at me. 'You never know what wonderful scene might suddenly arrive in front of you.' My hand in his, we walked across the beach: sand in my toes, feeling the green-glass charm on a thread around my neck beneath the swimsuit, and Rob beside me. I felt I was in heaven. And then it flicked through my mind — *Thanks, Nick, for telling me to treat myself to a holiday!*

We reached the cottage and stood looking at it for a moment, with its neglected slate roof, missing tiles, and windows broken by vandals or wild storms, I supposed — and the front door half-open, one latch hanging drunkenly down the side of the stone wall. Entering, we just stood there, gazing around us. My thoughts were all of Charles Mason painting here — there was a good north light — and waiting for Aunt Mary to arrive. And then? Of course they loved each other. The feeling inside the cobwebby, dusty little cottage told me so. I heaved a big sigh, and Rob looked at me anxiously.

'Something wrong, Goldie?' he asked. I shook my head.

'Just dreaming about the past,' I said, smiling at him. 'I think this was a sort of love nest.'

'Still could be.'

We looked at each other with laughing eyes, until he said, 'But those damned birds have to come first. Come with me this afternoon, Goldie?'

The spell was broken. I turned, went outside into the sun, and waited for him to join me.

'I'll drive us there, take the photographs, and then we could have a good meal somewhere before coming back. Okay with you?'

'And then back here for you with a

sleeping bag, and me in the spare bed just up on the cliff above.'

We looked at each other; then he took my hand and said gently, 'One thing at a time, Goldie. There's still so much to tell you, but not now. Now it's the birds. Come on, let's get going.'

The drive to the chough's nesting place was full of wonderful scenery, with the sea never far away. With Rob's camera at the ready, we walked over soft turf dotted with wild flowers until we reached the cliff edge. Here I tasted the saltiness on my lips, and the soft musical sound of waves far below filled me with pleasure. Here, with Rob, our kisses were still warm in my mind.

We sat down on a handy rock at the top of the cliff and waited, listening, watching. Very soon, they came — huge birds with powerful fringed wings. Their feathers were black, lightened with a dark blue and green gloss, and they had red curved beaks and strong red legs. 'Caio!' they called, and Rob and I caught our breaths because they were so spectacular and beautiful.

Rob stood up slowly and carefully. 'Wait here,' he whispered. 'I have to get nearer to them.'

I felt a sudden fear pierce me. What if he fell? What if, so busy focusing his camera, concentrating on composing a picture, he slipped and lost his footing? Oh, please, no. I couldn't bear it if he was injured. I held my breath, watching him. And then I remembered the green charm. I took it in my hands and stroked it, willing it to keep him safe. To look after him.

A few feet below me, he turned and smiled reassuringly. 'Amazing! There's a nest here with chicks, and the parents aren't keen on me getting any closer. But I must. What a picture it'll make. Right, here we go . . .'

I saw him stumbling as he neared the nest, and I knew the camera was heavy. Then suddenly something inside ordered me to be with him — to be there, should he fall. To watch him take so much trouble and expertise to get this amazing picture. Choughs and choughlets? I knew just what he was thinking — that this extraordinary picture might well be a competition winner.

Perhaps I had my mind taken off my feet for a few seconds. It all happened so quickly. My ankle turned on a small rock, my balance went, and I fell. Tumbling down, hitting rocks as I went down the cliffside, I know I screamed, forgetting the beauty of my surroundings, just feeling a wild longing to be safe.

Above me, I heard Rob's voice. 'Goldie! Try and grab a rock, or a bit of turf. Don't move, just stay there. I'm coming.'

I took huge breaths, felt my body all over, and discovered that I wasn't really hurt. A bruise or two, I was sure, but nothing broken. I stayed still as Rob had told me, and then he was beside me, feet slipping on the rocky ground. He bent over me and stared into my eyes, his face taut with anxiety. Then, seeing my own expression of relief, he let out his breath.

'Are you all right? Anything broken? How do you feel? Oh, Goldie — if anything had happened to you . . . ' His hands were about mine, moving over my body, pressing to see what damage I had sustained.

If anything had happened to you — and that desperate exhalation of relief. My bruises ceased to hurt and my shock dissolved, for surely he had said what was in his heart? I smiled at him and said calmly, 'No need to worry. I can move. If you help me, I'll get back up the cliff safely.'

He nodded, and I saw the fear fade from his face. He put his arms around me and gently pulled up until I was able to support myself. Then, still taking me with him, he turned and took a step up the rocky slope above us. Looking down at me as we struggled for balance, he said, 'When we're at the top, I'll phone for help. You need to get to hospital as soon as possible.'

By now I had got my breath back, and felt comfortingly safe. I said firmly, 'No, you won't. No need to go to hospital. I've only got a bruised knee and a scrape on one finger. Flo will be able to deal with that.'

We had reached the safety of soft turf and wild flowers. Birds cawed around us, and I wondered, just for a moment, if Rob had got the photo he wanted. But he was still looking anxiously at me, saying, 'No, I'm taking you to hospital, Goldie. A fall on a cliff isn't something you can just forget, you know.'

I surprised myself and him by laughing. 'But I *have* almost forgotten it. I'm safe, I'm unharmed and . . . ' I stopped short. Was this the time to tell him I knew he loved me? The expression on his face, his determination to rescue me, the strength of his warms arms — they all held a vital message, and I knew it to be his love for me that had made my escape possible. Yet something held me back. Could I just sit here with my hand bleeding and my leg aching, and ask him if he loved me?

Sitting there on the soft turf, with the music of the sea in my ears and the salt breeze on my lips, I knew this wasn't the time. I was simply grateful that I was safe, without serious injury. So I got up, stretched an aching leg, and smiled at him with determination and began walking — with a limp — to the car park.

'Goldie, are you sure you're all right?' He was still worried, and so I managed a bright smile.

'Of course I am. Go and get your camera — I suppose you left it by the nest? And then let's go back to Flo. I bet she's got a cupboard of old-fashioned ointments and weird medicine that will fit the bill.'

With the camera safely sitting on the back seat, we drove back to St Methyr. It was wonderful driving through the green lanes, and slowly my leg and grazed fingers began to ease. But the greatest comfort was still to come.

Parking outside Flo's cottage, Rob switched off the engine, turned to me and lifted my sore finger to his lips. 'What my mother used to say,' he said softly. 'A kiss will make it all better. Let's see, shall we?'

So without thinking any more, I leaned towards him and looked into his face. His eyes were clear and warm, and his lips as they came down on mine were surely a token of what he must feel for me. Could it mean that he loved me?

19

The next morning I slipped out of bed, assessed my injuries, and found that Flo's poultice and ointment had worked like a charm. But *my* charm — where was it? I fingered the small lump beneath my nightdress and smiled. It was here, keeping me safe. Had it been this charm, I wondered, that had given me Rob's gentle kisses before he left, making his way through the oncoming darkness, to sleep in the coastguard cottage?

The kisses had been wonderful, but had been interrupted by Flo bringing strong cups of tea to remedy my shock. 'Drink this,' she had ordered me. Then, turning to Rob, sitting on the bed, she added, 'And you too, lad. Goldie falling down a cliff wasn't what you expected, so drink up. Strong tea, my ma used to say, always does the trick.'

She left us then, but the kissing had

come to an end. 'Tomorrow I'll be around to see how you are, Goldie,' Rob said. 'There's another place I want to take you to, if you feel well enough. And you want to go shopping, you said.'

I ordered my mind to return to factual things, leaving dreams behind. 'Thank you, Rob. That all sounds good. And of course I'll be well enough.'

We looked at each other and smiled. But I knew he was thinking of today's reality, and I must just wait and be patient. 'What will you do today?' he asked, going towards the door with the empty mugs in his hands. 'Be careful, won't you? I don't want to find you in a heap on the floor when I get back this evening.'

I managed a small laugh. 'Don't worry. I'll wander about, walk along the beach, look at the cottage again. Eat Flo's large meals and think about those crazy choughs. Did you get a good photo of them?'

He nodded. 'Not bad. I'll send it into

the competition, but haven't got much hope. Too many experts out there, you see.'

What could I say? Nothing came into my mind, so I just said, 'Off you go then. And perhaps this evening you'll tell me where you're going to take me tomorrow. Sounds tantalising.'

His grin was clearly hiding something. But he simply took my hand, kissed my forehead, and said cheerily, 'Wait and see.'

I walked to the open window and watched as he drove away. It was a beautiful day, but without Rob to share it I felt subdued and disappointed. And then a voice I knew sounded from downstairs. Surely it couldn't be Gus? But yes, it was. I dressed in a hurry, brushed my hair and flew downstairs where I found him, sitting opposite Flo at the long pine table, laughing and drinking tea.

As I went into the room, Gus got up, looking at me and giving me that wonderful grin. He came across, put his arms around me, hugged me and landed a whiskery kiss on first one cheek and then the other. 'Good to see you, Goldie.' How pleased I was to hear that rough, deep voice. He went on, 'I hear you've been playing tricks and falling about and frightening the life out of Rob. What a silly thing to do! But you look fine. And that's good, because I'm planning to take you shopping.'

'Shopping?' My voice rose to a squeak. What on earth? And then I recalled Rob saying something about doing it. I gave him my warmest smile and said, 'I suppose Rob told you I wanted to buy a present for Aunt Mary?'

He nodded. 'He's too busy today to take you. Got a lot on his mind, poor lad, so he asked me to do it. Where are we going, then?'

I couldn't think straight for a moment. A lot on his mind? What could it be? The competition? Or something to do with me? Or perhaps not . . .

'Eat your breakfast,' Flo said, getting

out the frying pan, eggs and bacon and starting to cook. Of course Gus shared it. We sat around the table and I felt the world had taken a turn for the better.

Shopping with Gus was a real survival exercise. I reckoned his old car was as old, if not older, than he was; and despite the narrow lanes with invisible corners, he drove it as if he was taking part in a grand prix. I shut my eyes several times as we roared away from St Methyr and towards the next village. But there was an advantage to being with Gus. He knew the country-side. And more importantly, the local craftspeople who lived and worked here.

When he stopped in a quiet square, surrounded by trees and beside a flowing river, he looked at me and grinned. 'Here's where you'll find it, my dear.'

'Find what?'

'The present you're looking for. For your aunt. Just what she'll like, you'll see.'

We went into a small open-doored building, where there were noises and a strong scent of wood. 'You there, Tom?' asked Gus, and from the back of the room a man got to his feet, stared in surprise and then came across to us. He took Gus by the hand.

'Where you come from?' he asked. 'Not seen you fer years. And who's this young lady?'

Gus introduced me and then said, 'We're looking for something special, Tom. Can we have a look around?'

The man nodded, and with a wave of a calloused hand we started looking.

Everything was made of wood. Crafted, I should say. Tables of every size, chairs, delightful little jewelery boxes . . . and then my eye was caught by the row of photograph frames.

'Can I touch?' I asked, and Tom guffawed.

'Wouldn't sell nothing if I said no, would I? Here, let me reach a few down for you.'

They were smooth and polished,

thick and beautifully made. Frames of all sizes, and one particular one I could imagine holding one of Aunt Mary's special photos. Perhaps the one of Charles Mason outside his coastguard cottage. Yes, I was sure she would like that. I carried it to the counter, where Tom and Gus stood talking. A few words reached me, although my mind was fixed on Aunt Mary's present.

'Coming back, Gus? What, to live? And where?'

'Near St Methyr. A neglected old cottage that I'll enjoy bringing back to life.' Then, quickly, he turned and saw me clutching the frame. 'That looks a good present. Let Tom wrap it up for you and then we'll be on our way back. Mustn't be late.'

Briefly I wondered what that meant, but I was too busy complimenting the wood carver on his skill and paying for the frame. 'Come again,' said Tom, giving me a big smile as he handed over the package. 'Live locally, do you?'

I opened my mouth to tell him I lived

in Devon, but Gus cut into my words, saying, a note of amusement softening his voice, 'She might do, Tom. We'll have to see how it all works out.'

Before I could ask what on earth he meant, we were back in the car, racing towards Flo and the warm homely cottage, and I knew I was looking forward to a quiet, gossipy evening once Rob had returned. But Gus had one more mystery he planned to resolve. Getting out of the car, he took my hand, looked into my curious eyes, and said, 'Time for a walk, Goldie. There's somewhere I must take you.'

Flo looked at me and winked, and I wondered what all this secrecy was about. As we left the cottage, a car's headlights beamed over us. 'That's him,' said Gus happily. 'Just in time to come with us.'

Of course it was Rob, coming across to me after slamming the car door. He circled his arms around me, his voice quiet but full of what sounded like pleasure. He kissed me gently, and then turned to Gus, watching us. 'Does she know?' he asked in what was almost a whisper.

Gus shook his head. 'You're the one to tell her, lad. Not me. But we were just going up there — not too late, is it?'

'No.'

The one word, firm and determined, told me that whatever all this was about, it was important. And it concerned me. I turned to Rob. 'Come on, then,' I said huskily. 'Whatever it is, and wherever it might be, please let's go. This waiting and not knowing is driving me mad.' I put my arm through his, and then we started walking up towards the moonlit house on the cliff.

Small grey clouds slid slowly across the darkening red sky, but sunset colours still lit the horizon. The waves gave a soft shushing sound, and somewhere seagulls were still flying and calling. Some instinct told me this was a magic moment and must be treasured, no matter what might happen next. I stroked the green charm in my pocket and just waited, for I knew that the next few minutes were perhaps the most important in my life.

Rob's arm around my waist was warm and strong, and beside me Gus's heavy footsteps were a reassurance of some kind. As we neared the house on the cliff, Rob suddenly came to a halt. Gus went on walking, but Rob looked at me; and when he broke the silence, his voice was quiet and a bit unsteady. 'Goldie,' he said huskily, 'my darling Goldie, do you think you'd be happy to live here? In Cliff House?' A pause, and then the magic question I had so longed to hear. 'With me?'

I had no words. My heart was racing. My arms wound around his neck, and I kissed him. We stayed like that until we ran out of breath, and then we parted, looking at each other, smiling, trying to think of things to say, but knowing that all we wanted was to go on kissing. Until Rob's arms slipped down, and he took my hand and started leading me up the rough path towards Cliff House. Closing the gate behind us, he smiled, saying, 'Was that your answer? Please, Goldie, tell me. You see, I'm asking you to change your life — no more office to work in, an old house to run, and me to cope with.'

I paused, hearing the gate swing shut, and said unsteadily, 'Darling Rob, all of that is what I want most in the world. Yes, please — and yes!'

Another kiss, and then we both decided that we were here for a reason. We went up through the garden, and he produced the key to the front door. Waiting, I stood in a shaft of moonlight that filtered through the hurrying clouds, and felt truly happy.

There were footsteps just behind us, and turning, I saw Gus. He beamed in the half-light and said, 'All decided, is it? I gave you enough time, I hope?'

We all laughed as we went into the dark house. Rob switched on the hall light and looked around him. Then he turned. 'Yes, Gus, it was just about enough time, though we could have done with more.' Again we laughed, but then his voice changed. 'Time now, I think, to tell Goldie exactly what happened and why we're here. Let's go through into the garden room — we'll still have some light there.'

The garden room was delightful — a wide, spacious glass chamber with comfortable chairs, and a variety of plants lining the wall and climbing up a pole erected in the middle of the room. 'Jasmine,' I said softly. 'My favourite plant. Just smell it!'

We sat down. Rob moved his chair nearer to mine, and Gus sat, legs akimbo, in the biggest chair he could find. Well?' he said, and that was the start of the saga he and Rob were about to unfold.

'You know the muddle about the inheritance of my father's will, Goldie?'

'Yes, Rob — and I thought it was all cleared up now, once you had notice of your father's death? The inheritance divided between you and Gus?'

Rob nodded and held out his hand towards me. I enclosed it in both of mine and smiled at him. 'Well, go on, then,' I murmured.

He sighed. 'The one thing you didn't know was that my father owned Cliff House. It's to be shared between Gus and me.'

For a moment I was worried. Did he mean that Gus would be living here with us here in Cliff House? I was fond of Gus, of course I was — but Rob and I needed a place of our own.

I looked at him and saw he was smiling. I knew he understood. Then he looked at Gus and said warmly, 'Your turn now to take up the tale, please.'

Gus fidgeted in the big chair and then cleared his throat. Well,' he said in his deep voice, 'I'm going to live in the coastguard cottage. All part of the estate, you see, and badly in need of doing up. I'll enjoy that. And once it's liveable, I'll get out my paints and make some more daubs.' He sat upright and looked across at me, and I saw the warm expression on his face. 'What do you think about that? Can you agree with an old fellow like me making a new start?' His voice lowered and his smile grew. 'Back in the home he loved so much when he was just a lad?'

I felt tears threatening, but I blinked them away, holding out my hand to him and feeling joyful about how all this confusing business was working out. Unsteadily I said, 'It's a dream coming true, Gus. I'm happy for you that you can share it.'

And then I remembered that Flo had always kept a small cellar next door to the kitchen. Would there be a bottle there that we could celebrate with? There was, and so we sat in the garden room until Gus got to his feet and said, 'I must get back to my B and B down in the village, or they'll wonder where I've got to. But tomorrow I'll be in the cottage and start the good work.'

H stood up a bit stiffly, came over and kissed me. He held out his hand to Rob and they smiled at each other. At the doorway he turned and grinned at us. 'Goodnight, you two lovebirds.' He chuckled. 'Well, who knows what that competition will bring, eh?' And he went off. We heard the front door quietly shut, and then Rob and I were alone.

He took me in his arms, looked into my shining eyes and said quietly, 'I'll walk you home, sweetheart. A stroll along the beach, do you think?'

I could think of nothing better. We left Cliff House and took the small path down to the moonlit beach. And there, listening to the music of the waves curling at our feet, I knew I had to do something important. I took the green charm, and together we looked into its gleaming centre.

Rob said, 'It worked, didn't it? All that magic.'

'Yes,' I answered. 'And now it must go back to where it came from. Perhaps waiting for another person to find it again.'

He nodded and watched as I said

goodbye to the green charm and threw it back into the sea. Was it just imagination that made me think I saw a huge splash as it sank? I took a deep breath. It was over. Rob led me back to Flo's cottage,where she waited with the kettle humming on the hob and a warm smile on her lined face. Then Rob set off for the coastguard cottage where he would sleep, and we kissed before he went.

'Sleep well, my darling,' he said, and the warmth in his voice lit up my thoughts.

Our lives had changed. There were still be problems to be resolved, but I knew without any doubt that we would manage to do so. Together.

20

Of course there were problems. And the first one I must face was telling Nick I was definitely leaving the business, and going to live in Cornwall. Reaching for the phone, I expected shouts and explosions; but when he had heard me out, he just said, 'You can't leave, Goldie. I have another idea, you see. We'll expand the business into Cornwall and you can run it. How about that?'

'What?' I thought hard. Maybe that was a good, workable idea. For a second I saw myself in the new office, answering the phone. *Marigold Smith speaking, of the Nick Burns Holiday Lets Agency. How can I help you?* I was grinning as I said, 'Wonderful, Nick! I'd love to do that. Thank you so much for suggesting it.'

'My pleasure,' he said, and then, drily

and with amusement, I thought, 'You'll be glad to know that the new woman — ' He paused before adding with a chuckle, ' — my *niece*, is doing well and loves working with me. So how's that for a surprise, then?'

'Yes, Nick, it all sounds good.' I thought for a minute. 'You remember that Cliff House was a holiday let? Now it's my home, with Rob.'

Another chuckle. 'So it was the bird man after all, was it? I hope you'll be happy, Goldie. You deserve to be.'

'Thank you,' I said gratefully. Another pause, and then I said, 'So I'll set up my new office, shall I, and start looking around for more good old houses with owners who want to rent out?'

Nick laughed. 'You've got it all worked out, Goldie, just as I knew you would. Well, cheers for now, and I'll be in touch soon. I'll send you the latest enquiries and you can have fun dealing with them. Quite a lot off my shoulders. Bless you, Goldie.'

I breathed deeply. This was not what

I had expected, but it was a wonderful answer to the idea of leaving work.

After lunch, I walked along the beach. Rob had already left, with a new commission to illustrate a book being written about Cornwall with bird illustrations. We were both delighted with such good news, but as I reminded him before he went off that morning, we must be back in Exeter in time for Aunt Mary's birthday on Friday.

'Don't worry, darling,' he said. 'Gus says you've bought a suitable present, and we'll be there for the celebratory tea.' He looked along the cliff. 'So what's Gus up to?'

I laughed. 'What do you think? Getting the cottage into good enough shape for him to move into. Do you think he could do with a bit of help? I'm good at painting walls.'

'Leave him to do it his way,' said Rob, with a twinkle in his eyes. 'But when you see him, suggest he comes back for your aunt's birthday, will you? I bet he'd love to come with us.'

And so it was all arranged. I found Gus removing damp wallpaper from an interior wall and offered to help, but as I expected, he preferred to do it all himself. 'That's kind of you, my dear, but no thanks. This is a work of love, you see. Being back here, among all the memories.'

I kissed him and went on my way. Gus would always be a man who lived his life exactly as he wanted to. I just hoped that once the cottage was liveable, he would unpack his paints and think about those 'daubs'.

Later that afternoon, having looked at the room I fancied as my new office, I said goodbye to Flo and promised I would be down again next week, once the famous birthday was over. As I drove into Torquay, I knew the next problem was trying to sell my flat. This was a bad time for selling property, but the problems seemed to be resolving themselves well, so perhaps someone would soon look at the flat and think, 'Yes, I'll buy this.'

I spent the next few days packing up, and also shopping for what I knew I would need at Cliff House. I guessed Flo was waiting to help me, which was a calming thought. I wondered what I could give her for all the help she had offered lately, and finally thought I would buy her seeds for her little garden. She would love that.

I walked around the attractive parts of Torquay and bade them goodbye. Then I headed for Exeter and Aunt Mary's home at Riverside.

Matron greeted me. 'Good to see you, Marigold.' She led me upstairs and paused by Aunt Mary's closed door. 'May I suggest that you come to luncheon and stay on for the tea party?'

'I'd love that, Matron. And I'm sure the party will be wonderful.'

'Well, we've got the balloons, and the cake is being made — and of course your aunt will expect her telegram from the Queen.' She knocked at the door and opened it. 'Mrs Seaton, here's your niece.' With a smile she left the room, and I hugged Aunt Mary and kissed her cheek.

'My dear Marigold! So lovely to see you. Now, do tell me what you've been doing, away in Cornwall. Donna Adams called last night and said you and Rob were there.'

I thought, *Oh dear. What did she call for, I wonder?*

But Aunt Mary's smile grew. 'She brought back the photos of the Crosby girls that she borrowed for the exhibition. Such a kind thought. And so I invited her to tea on Friday. How lovely it will be, with all my family and friends around me.'

I nodded, realising that it was indeed kind of Donna to bother to return the photos. And I would make her welcome at the party — I grinned to myself — now that I knew she and Rob didn't care for each other. 'Who else is coming? Anyone I know?'

Aunt Mary gave another smile that showed her dimples. 'That nice man, your boss, who was so kind to me at the exhibition. Mr Burns, I think he's called. He'll be here.'

I looked at the portrait of the three girls, now returned to the wall behind Aunt Mary's chair, and thought what a lot had happened — was still happening — since we first learned who they were and how they had lived.

Now the days seemed to rush past. So many things to do! Rob had taken his photographs for the first chapter of the new book, and was here for a day or so. And then, of course, it would be Friday. I told him who was coming to the party, and he grinned when I mentioned Nick Burns.

'My rival,' he said with a laugh, and I put my arms around him.

'You never had a rival,' I told him, joining in the laughter.

We went to see Gus, who had returned from his labours in Cornwall and was sprucing himself up for the party. 'It was good of your aunt to invite me,' he said, holding up a new dark red jersey he intended to surprise everybody with on Friday. 'And I'm seeing the hairdresser,' he added, eyes twinkling. 'Hair and beard — you won't know me.'

I put my arms around him and whispered, 'Don't change too much, dear Gus. It's you we love, not your appearance.' He nodded at me, and I saw his eyes shining.

At last Friday dawned. I was up early, putting a few more things into boxes, ready for the big move to Cornwall. But I found time to wash my hair and put on a favourite linen trouser suit, smart enough for a party, I thought. Honey-coloured, it made my hair shine; and with high-heeled shoes that matched the small clutch bag I carried, I looked at my reflection in the mirror. 'Not bad,' I told myself, and then with a smile set off for luncheon with Aunt Mary.

The birthday girl was bright and full of smiles, and ate her special meal of roast lamb and red currant jelly with a good appetite. She got stuck a bit with the chocolate mousse and clotted cream, but after luncheon was over and she had gone back to her room for a short nap, she was herself again, as we took her down to the drawing room, decorated and full of friends and family. Beneath the balloons and posters of 'happy birthday', we gathered for an hour and chatting amongst ourselves, passing around the telegram from the Queen, and making sure Aunt Mary was enjoying herself and not getting too tired.

Rob brought Gus along, and Nick appeared. I gave the photo frame to Aunt Mary, and then Rob asked what she would like to put in it. She looked at the sheaf of photos he offered and said, 'I'd like to have the picture of Charles Mason standing outside Coast-guard Cottage.' There was silence while Rob fitted the photo into the frame, and we all smiled as, holding it, she added, almost to herself, 'I can look at this every day — and remember.'

Then the huge colourful cake was

brought in, and the one candle lit and blown out among laughter and good wishes. Matron said a few words, and there was a call for Aunt Mary to reply.

I held her hand as she sat up straighter. Her voice was uneven, but her smile told us how happy she was. 'Thank you,' she said. 'Thank you all. What a wonderful day. And even if I live another hundred years, I know the next birthday can never be as good as this one.'

There was applause, and then the room started to empty. Aunt Mary was taken back to the comfortable chair in her room, with the picture of Charles Mason on her lap. Rob and I kissed her good-bye. She looked up at us and smiled as she said, 'I do believe Cornwall's magic has made you two happy. Now you're together, bless you both.'

As we left Riverside, Rob found a piece of paper in his car with large scribbled words that I was sure were from Gus. The message was short. 'You've won the competition! Your photo of the eagle, my boy. Nice things have been said about it, and there's a promise for more work in the future. Well done.'

Rob looked at me with wide, sparkling eyes. 'How about that?' he said, and we both laughed before stepping close and kissing. I felt pride and such happiness, and then Rob whispered, 'Goldie, I can never be thankful enough for finding you. You've given me happiness as well as your amazing love. Maybe your glass charm really did work some magic.'

I nodded. Thoughts danced around in my head, and then something made me say, 'It was the Crosby girls who brought us together, Rob — showing me that love is something rare and beautiful. And we're so lucky to share it.'

We drove back to The Studio; and I knew that in a minute Gus wold come in, and we would celebrate what the charm — and the Crosby girls — had brought into our lives.

We do hope that you have enjoyed reading this large print book.

Did you know that all of our titles are available for purchase?

We publish a wide range of high quality large print books including:
Romances, Mysteries, Classics
General Fiction
Non Fiction and Westerns

Special interest titles available in large print are:
The Little Oxford Dictionary
Music Book, Song Book
Hymn Book, Service Book

Also available from us courtesy of Oxford University Press:
Young Readers' Dictionary
(large print edition)
Young Readers' Thesaurus
(large print edition)

For further information or a free brochure, please contact us at:
Ulverscroft Large Print Books Ltd.,
The Green, Bradgate Road, Anstey,
Leicester, LE7 7FU, England.
Tel: (00 44) 0116 236 4325
Fax: (00 44) 0116 234 0205

Other titles in the
Linford Romance Library:

BLUEPRINT FOR LOVE

Henriette Gyland

Hazel Dobson is pleased when she gets temp work at Gough Associates, an architectural company based in a beautiful manor house in Norfolk. While it's a far cry from the bright lights of London, she is keen to get away from a mundane job with a lecherous boss, and to spend some time with her great-aunt. There she meets handsome and wealthy Jonathan Gough, and sees a chance at happiness and a family with him. But some people just don't want Hazel and Jonathan to be happy . . .

LAKELAND INTERLUDE

Jean M. Long

Following a painful break-up, Casey Brett decides to start a new life in the Lake District as an assistant in her friend Flora's Dance and Drama Studio. But it's not all plain sailing, as a fellow instructor feels Casey is stepping on her toes, she receives the unwanted romantic attentions of a local hiking guide, and she loses several of her most promising students. But she also meets wealthy businessman Blake Lawley, and feels an instant frisson. Can Casey overcome her problems and find happiness in her new home?